A SCOT MESS

A COMEDY OF ERRORS

CAROLINE LEE

COPYRIGHT

ABOUT THIS BOOK

Laird Oliphant's sons have no choice but to get married.

Without an heir, the laird has gathered his sons—his six *illegitimate* sons, all born in the same year—and declared whoever presents him with a grandson first, will become the next Highland Laird.

Reactions are...*mixed.*

But to Finn Oliphant, this is exactly the news he's been hoping for. You see, Finn has already chosen his future wife: the vivacious and intelligent Fiona MacIan, whom he fell in love with the previous year. He knows she's in love with him as well, so this whole "marriage ultimatum" thing should be easy-peasy. He'll simply invite Fiona to Oliphant Castle to sign all the betrothal contracts and... *Bam*! Done! They can get on with the baby-making!

Except...

It's not that Fiona is getting cold feet, exactly. She's fairly certain she loves Finn. Mostly. Well, verra likely, at least. But she's never been the most self-confident woman, especially compared to her sister—her *identical twin* sister—whom Finn happens to mistake for Fiona upon their arrival at his keep, which is *super*-awkward all around.

The idea of marrying Finn makes her feel all warm and giddy—hopefully that's just lust, not the ague—but how can she be certain he truly wants *her*, and not just *any* woman?

It's hard enough to be certain of anything on Oliphant land, especially with Finn's mad Aunt Agatha spreading rumors, five potential brothers-in-law offering terrible advice, and a mysterious ghostly drummer keeping the entire keep awake at all hours.

And *mayhap* Finn should've mentioned *his* identical twin brother as well? That information likely would have saved everyone a lot of headache...and a lot of heartbreak.

Finn and Fiona have plenty to learn about themselves, and one another, before they can be certain this marriage is a good idea. But unfortunately, they're running out of time. Dun-dun-duuuuuuuun!

Warning... This comedy of errors is not for anyone who can't handle the following: plenty of naughty scenes, more than a few anachronistic jokes, and an embarrassing number of mistaken-identity gags. Only pick up this book if you have a sense of humor. You've been warned.

OTHER BOOKS BY CAROLINE LEE

Want the scoop on new books? Join Caroline's Cohort, an exclusive reader group! Or sign up for my mailing list by texting "Caroline" to 42828 to get started!

Steamy Scottish Historicals:
The Sinclair Jewels (4 books)
The Highland Angels (5 books)
The Hots for Scots (8 books)
Highlander Ever After (3 books)
Bad in Plaid (6 books)

Sensual Historical Westerns:
Black Aces (3 books)
Sunset Valley (3 books)
Everland Ever After (10 books)
The Sweet Cheyenne Quartet (6 books)

Sweet Contemporary Westerns
Quinn Valley Ranch (5 books)
River's End Ranch (14 books)
The Cowboys of Cauldron Valley (7 books)

The Calendar Girls' Ranch (6 books)

Click **here** to find a complete list of Caroline's books.

*Sign up for Caroline's Newsletter to receive exclusive content and freebies, as well as first dibs on her books! Or if newsletters aren't your thing, follow her on **Bookbub** for a quick, concise new release alert every time she publishes a book!*

PROLOGUE

THE MOMENT he'd set eyes on her, he'd known she was someone special.

He had been passing through the marketplace at Wick, having finished his transaction, and was heading for a tavern for supper, which had been recommended by the merchant he'd just been haggling with. Finn Oliphant was hungry and his steps were determined.

But hearing her voice stopped him in his tracks.

She had been arguing with a cloth seller for a bolt of green velvet. She'd been confident and certain of her righteousness as she haggled, and that sense of surety in her voice had piqued his interest.

But when she'd turned, triumphantly struggling with the cloth she now owned, he'd found himself instantly lost in the sparkle of those perfect blue eyes.

Offering to help her with the heavy bolt had been instinctual, and by the time he'd walked her to the wagon she'd brought to market, he was half in love.

Despite her status as a laird's sister, Fiona MacIan was not proud or haughty. She and her guard—an older man, who had the most unusual method of cursing—traveled weekly to surrounding markets to suss out the best deals for the MacIans' limited coin.

Over meat pies, once she agreed to join him for supper, she and Finn had swapped stories and laughter over the many deals they'd made with merchants, mostly to their advantages.

He'd been utterly captivated by her zest for life, her willingness to work, and her complete selflessness. She'd blushed prettily when he'd complimented her, and when he'd kissed her, she'd responded exactly the way he'd hoped.

They'd managed to avoid her guard for the rest of the evening and had spent the time wrapped in each other's arms in the hayloft of the tavern's stables.

Oh, Finn hadn't compromised her, despite how desperately aroused she'd made him...but they'd spent the time learning about one another's pasts, tasting one another's lips, and planning for a future together.

The next day, Fiona twisted in her seat at the front of the wagon to blow him a kiss as she headed away from Wick.

Finn had stood there in the road, watching her until she was out of sight. He suspected he *should* feel sad, *should* feel bereft, knowing winter would be upon them soon and chances to travel would be limited.

But he felt none of those things.

Instead, his heart was soaring, *flying*.

Despite his lack of release last night, he'd never spent a happier time in a woman's arms.

Aye, Fiona MacIan was heading away from him, but that mattered not.

Because, *somehow*, he was going to make that woman his wife.

CHAPTER 1

LAIRD OLIPHANT'S sons were hungover.

At least, most of them were.

Finn certainly was. He currently had his chin propped up on his fist, his elbow resting on the trestle table in the great hall, and was attempting to do the math.

Alistair wasn't hungover, of course, because the man never took the time away from his work to have any fun. That was one. And 'twas hard to tell with Malcolm, their most scholarly brother. *He* was muttering to himself as he doodled designs for something—an innovative new ploughshare? A siege weapon? A brooch for Duncan to smith?—in the spilled ale in front of him.

So that was two of the brothers, leaving four.

Finn squinted, trying to ignore the growing noise as the household woke for the day.

Six minus two *was* four, aye?

Aye.

He blew out a breath, wishing he had some ale for his parched throat. Or water, barring aught else.

So aye, it would be factual to state that *most* of Laird Oliphant's sons were hungover.

But of course, they had no proof there weren't *more* sons out there somewhere. Da prided himself on having gathered all of his known bastards under his roof, making sure they were raised right. And he'd always said that, after siring *three* sets of twins in less than a year, he'd vowed to keep his cock tucked inside his kilt where it belonged.

Right up until that disastrous marriage of his, at least.

"What has ye looking so suspicious?"

Finn startled, then winced when the movement sent a spike of pain through his forehead. Scowling, he turned to his twin.

"What?"

Duncan's head was propped against the stone wall behind him, and he scowled right back. "Ye're glaring at the world as if"—he paused to swallow, his voice even more gravelly than usual—"as if the ghostly drummer of Oliphant Castle is banging on the inside of yer skull. Or as if ye've come up with a scheme to save us from Da's ultimatum."

Save them?

When Da had handed him the means to achieve his fondest wish?

Finn stopped himself before he could snort in derision, knowing it wouldn't help his head.

"Nay." He finally managed to make his tongue work properly. "I mean, *aye*, the drummer *is* pounding inside my head."

Duncan's eyes closed. "He was pounding all last night too. Did ye no' hear him? By St. Simon's left earlobe, 'tis annoying. Cannae even leave a man to bemoan his fate in peace."

Despite his headache, Finn's brows lifted in surprise.

Dunc had heard the drummer?

Not everyone did, but Finn had heard him so often over the last half-year, he thought he was the only one doomed to have disrupted sleep.

"I was—" Wait, what *had* Finn been thinking of? Oh, aye. "I was doing maths."

"God help us, he's doing maths," came a groan from his other side.

Rocque was lying face-down, his head in his arms. Finn hadn't realized their largest brother was awake, much less cognizant.

He poked the man. "Was that ye, Rocque?"

"Nay," Rocque mumbled. "No' if ye're doing maths."

It was Malcolm who answered his twin, offering a teasing grin as he looked up from his doodles. "Come now, Rocque, we've been over this. Mathematics isnae to be feared. 'Tis a useful skill, and one ye use every day." He shifted forward on his bench, propping his elbows on either side of his smeared drawing and lacing his fingers together. "Two bannock cakes plus two bannock cakes makes—"

"A man no' shit for a week?" Finn supplied.

Malcolm's eyes crinkled as he tried not to smile. "And if Kiergan has six women who are willing to fook him senseless, and there are seven days in a week, how many women can he—"

"Shut up, Mal," Rocque growled, not lifting his head from his arms.

Duncan pushed himself upright. "One each night?" he offered.

"Excellent!" Malcolm beamed. "And none on Sunday, which is the Lord's Day."

"Aye, nae fornicating on the Lord's Day." Finn elbowed his twin in the side. " 'Tis for loving yer own hand."

Duncan rolled his eyes, then winced and dropped his head to his hand. " 'Tis the only loving we're likely to have, if Da has his way."

"Oh, for Christ's sake, he wants ye to marry, no' become celibate." Kiergan's words drifted up from the bench on the other side of Malcolm. "There *is* a difference."

Finn stretched forward, but even then could only see his brother's cocked knee where it rested against the table. "I was wondering where ye'd gone."

"From the pounding of my head, I'd say Hell," Kiergan muttered.

"What in damnation do ye mean, *he wants* ye *to marry?*" Rocque finally lifted his head from the table. "Are ye no' one of his sons? Were ye no' included in his order?"

One of Kiergan's fingers rose above the table. "Ah, but ye see, 'tis where we differ. *I* have nae intention of following said orders."

Rocque snorted and reached across the table, grabbing the flagon of ale from beside his twin. "Good luck," he muttered, before lifting the drink to his lips.

"Have ye no' had enough?" Malcolm asked, his teasing turning to concern.

All the Oliphants knew this particular set of twins were the closest, even though they couldn't be more dissimilar. They'd come into the laird's care the latest, having been raised until the age of twelve by a distant relative, who wanted naught to do with the lads.

They'd been accepted with open arms by William Oliphant's other bastard sons, but scholarly Malcolm and bull-chested Rocque had a special bond.

But, God love him, Malcolm apparently didn't know the best cure for a hangover.

" 'Twill do him good," Finn said, reaching for the flagon and pulling it away from Rocque. "And me too."

Greedily, he drank down the ale, relishing in the way the cool liquid eased his dry throat. But when Dunc nudged him, Finn sighed into the mug and passed the ale to his twin, knowing the poor man needed it more than him.

After all, Duncan—*all* of them—had just found out they had to marry, and soon.

Last night, after supper, Da had bid Nessa goodnight and sent her up to her chambers, citing her recent loss as part of his command. Their sister had glared at them all, but when Da had refused to relent, she'd huffed mightily and stomped upstairs, shooed along by daft Aunt Agatha. Then Da had turned to all of them.

"Well, my lads," he'd begun, in that great booming voice of his, "ye ken I have nae legitimate sons, and I refuse to allow that sniveling cousin of mine the lairdship after I'm gone. 'Twill have to be one of ye."

All six of them had sat straight up in their seats at that, exchanging glances. Alistair had looked intrigued, but then, he'd always been more interested in running the clan than the rest of them. Duncan had looked horrified; Rocque interested; Malcolm concerned; and Kiergan…?

Well, Kiergan had burst out laughing.

"How will ye choose, Da?" the rakish brother of theirs had called out, lifting his ale in salute. "And how will ye convince the clan to accept one of us?"

William Oliphant had smiled then, a chilling smile, which told Finn he had a plan.

A smile which *should've* told them what was coming. A smile which *should've* warned them they wouldn't like his meddling.

" 'Tis simple, lads," Da had said casually, leaning back in his great wooden chair. "Ye'll all marry before the summer's over. The first one of ye to present me with a grandson will be the next chieftain."

Kiergan had quit laughing then.

The arguments had been over quickly, when it was clear Da wasn't joking. He intended them all to marry and start producing bairns for him to bounce on his knee, and the first one with a son would become laird.

Finn doubted he was the only one of the six Oliphant bastards who was wondering if he *wanted* a son.

Or a lairdship.

However, he *knew* he was the only one who had been pleased by Da's decision, because now Finn had a path to the future he wanted.

Marriage to Fiona MacIan.

So when Da had made his escape, and the whisky had started flowing, Finn hadn't been mourning his lost bachelorhood, nay. But he'd always been an affable sort and had wanted to support his brothers in their misery.

At least, that's what he'd told himself.

When the cock had crowed that morning, he'd wondered if mayhap it'd been ill-advised to drink so heavily.

But now that his throat was cooled, and the smell of porridge wafted from the undercroft and kitchens, Finn decided he didn't feel all that bad after all.

"Are ye lads ready to break yer fast?"

Moira, the housekeeper, stood behind Malcolm, holding a tray, one brow cocked disapprovingly. When Rocque groaned, one corner of her lips pulled up.

"I brought simple bread and water, but I could be convinced to fetch ye some poached fish. In berry sauce. And oysters. And jellied eels. And some fragrant aged cheese to—"

"Cease, woman!" Duncan called, dropping his head into his hands once more. "For the love of God, only bread, please."

Smirking openly now, Moira leaned over Kiergan to thump the tray in front of them. "Only bread? Nae oysters or eel sauce or elderberry jam?"

Beside Finn, Rocque made an ill noise and lowered his forehead to his arms again. Malcolm, however, smiled brightly up at the plump woman who'd fussed over all of them since they'd arrived at Oliphant Castle.

"Thank ye, dear Moira," he said politely, grabbing a hunk of the bread and tossing another to Finn. "Ye heard of our fate?"

The way the housekeeper nodded made Finn wonder—as he bit into the warm brown bread—if she'd known Da's plans before the rest of them.

"I think 'tis a fine idea, although the laird makes a dangerous wager."

"Aye," Finn agreed. "He might end up with Kiergan as the next Oliphant."

"*Never!*" came the impassioned claim from the bench. "I'll no' jump to marry some lass just because Da dangles a prize I dinnae even want in front of my nose!" His hand rose again, reaching for the table. "Now, one of ye louts pass me some of that bread."

Moira nudged the bench with her knee. "Why no' sit up and join the rest of the living?"

"Because," Kiergan groaned, "I dinnae think my back is working this morning, and my head is much more comfortable lying here. Ale, please?"

As Finn broke off a piece of the bread and passed it to his twin—

Duncan snatched it out of his hand with a grateful grunt, but didn't lift his head—Moira caught the eye of a serving wench.

"Ale here, Minnie! And if any of these clot-heids pinch yer bottom, remind them they're to be married soon!"

As Rocque groaned again, Kiergan shook his finger at the woman they all viewed as a second mother—those that still had mothers in the first place, at least.

"Woman, ye would take away all our fun? For an edict which hasnae come to pass yet?"

"Aye," Moira agreed cheerfully. "Ye'll all be married by Hogmany, and our laird will get his grandbairns!"

Bairns…

The thought of Fiona's belly swelling with his child made Finn smile.

He was so distracted, he almost didn't notice Moira bend down and reach for the bench where Kiergan lay. With one great heave, she sent the man to the floor with a heavy thud.

His curses mixed with her laughter as she sauntered away. And when Minnie arrived with the ale, Finn noticed none of his brothers made any move to touch her.

By the time the rest of the household was awake and bustling about, Finn's headache was completely gone. He was listening to Malcolm explain his doodle—apparently a set of reflecting mirrors with which to view objects far away—and wishing he had some of the porridge he saw the serving wenches hurrying about with.

On one side, Duncan seemed to be feeling better, but 'twas hard to tell with him. Finn's twin had never been the most emotive of men, and Da's news had sent him into a permanent scowl. Years of living with the man had taught Finn to give him his distance and not tease him much.

Rocque, in typical fashion, had perked up once the food was delivered, and was on his second loaf already. He didn't say much, but listened to his twin's idea without interrupting.

It was Kiergan whose mood hadn't improved with the arrival of food. In fact, he was nursing another flagon of ale already, frowning morosely into the depths, as if the liquid held the secret to his escape.

"Ye ken what we need?" this rakish brother of theirs interrupted Malcolm's explanation.

When they all turned to Kiergan, no doubt wondering if he'd found a way to counter Da's edict, he swirled the ale in his mug.

"Ye're the inventor, Malcolm," Kiergan said thoughtfully, "surely ye could come up with some sort of—I dinnae ken—*drink* for us to take in the mornings, when our heads feel like wool."

"Aye," Rocque grunted. "'Something to wake us up and give us energy."

"Sounds addicting," Malcolm said blandly. "Where would I get the ingredients to make this magic drink?"

"Beans."

When everyone shifted their attention to Duncan, the taciturn man shrugged and repeated, "*Magic* beans?"

Malcolm hummed, his eyes already focusing on the wall behind Finn's head. "So we take these magic beans and grind them up...and then what? Mayhap pour some hot water over them? To soak out the magic, I suppose. Then we drink that water and it gives us energy and wipes away the ill-effects of too much ale..."

Kiergan nodded. "Get on that, Mal. All ye need is to find the source of the magic beans."

"Aye," Rocque agreed. "But that doesnae solve our current dilemma."

The reminder dropped the rest of them into silence once more, each focused on their mugs or bread, and each likely thinking of what the future would bring.

"Ye lads look like yer favorite horse died!"

Finn jerked at the sound of their father's greeting, and from the way the ale sloshed over Kiergan's cup, he wasn't the only one surprised by his sudden presence.

Despite the fact they were seated along one wall, rather than the high table, Da joined them when Malcolm shifted over to give him room.

"Good morrow, Da."

"*Is* it a good one? Because Kiergan is clearly mourning."

Malcolm shrugged and passed his father his own flagon of ale. "Kiergan doesnae see the possibilities."

William Oliphant peered at his scholarly son. "And ye do?"

Glancing down at the imaginary sketch he'd made on the wooden table, Malcolm shrugged again. "I am one of six bastards, Da. No' the strongest, nor the bravest."

"Ye're the smartest though," Rocque said, through a mouthful of bread.

A smile flitted across Malcolm's face, before disappearing. "Likely, but I had nae intention of lairdship."

"Aye," their father said gently, shifting forward to plant his elbows on the table in a manner eerily similar to Duncan's. "But I also ken ye had thoughts of joining the Church at one point."

"I'm too auld now," Malcolm pointed out, "although I'd give my eyeteeth to study at the Abbey."

"So ye dinnae begrudge my orders? Ye'll marry and sire a son for the good of the Oliphants?"

Malcolm's brows dipped in, the way they did when he was thinking. "I understand ye had to issue the order to *all* of us, or one would weasel out of it."

Kiergan grunted. "I'll *still* find a way to weasel out of it."

"Ye're the most talented weasel of us all," Rocque agreed.

"Go jump off a cliff," Kiergan snapped.

The largest Oliphant bastard laughed in reply.

It was Duncan who dragged them back to the conversation. "So ye'll do it, Mal? Ye'll find a wench and marry her?"

"I'll find a *mother* and marry her."

When both Duncan and Rocque grunted in question, Malcolm elaborated.

"Ye see, lads, the trick to success is no' falling in love with a pretty face, like Finn here, but contracting a marriage with a woman who is already a proven breeder."

Da hummed thoughtfully. "So yer plan is to find a widow with sons?"

"Aye, which proves she's already successfully carried a male child to term." Malcolm nodded proudly.

For the first time, Kiergan looked up from his ale with something other than anger in his eyes. His snort was incredulous as he shook his head. "*Breeder*? Ye clearly have *nae idea* how to woo a woman, do ye, brother?"

"Woo her?" Malcolm shook his head. "I'm contracting marriage, no' building a lifelong love."

"Women are complicated," Rocque growled, reaching across the table for Kiergan's abandoned loaf of bread. "She'll no' like ye thinking of her as naught more than a breeder."

Finn nodded, knowing Rocque's disagreements with his hot-tempered, long-term mistress—the village midwife and healer—were legendary. "Ye have to use a bit of charm, Mal, if ye want to be happy."

"Charm." Kiergan rolled his eyes. "Listen to the man. He kens all there is to ken about women, eh?"

Not offended by his brother's teasing, Finn crossed his arms in front of his chest and leaned back against the stone wall behind him. "There's a difference between bedding a woman and loving one, Kiergan. When ye meet the right one—"

Every man at the table—including Da—joined in on the refrain. "*Ye'll just ken it, like a bolt from above.*"

Mayhap he'd told the story before, but Fiona was one of Finn's favorite topics, and he wasn't going to let it go so easily. "She'll make ye go all warm, and yer heart will hurt to think of being apart from her."

" 'Tis lust, no' love," Kiergan muttered as he lifted his flagon. "And ye sound as mad as Aunt Agatha."

But Da was grinning. "So ye're no' angered by my demand?"

"I think 'tis high-handed and domineering," Finn answered with a smile, "but I cannae be angered, because 'tis exactly what I've been wanting."

Before Da could respond, their sister Nessa stepped up beside him and placed a bowl of porridge in front of the older man. "Is Finn going on about his love again?"

"Thank ye, lass."

Da nodded to his only legitimate child and offered his cheek for a kiss, which she obliged, then moved to sit on the opposite end of the bench, scooting alongside Kiergan, who hurried to place the ale down on the table and turn a concerned look upon his sister.

"How are ye feeling, lass?"

For all of his women, all of his conquests, Finn knew Kiergan kept a special place in his heart for Nessa. Of all the brothers, Kiergan and Alistair had been raised in the keep since birth. They'd been there through Da's disastrous marriage and Nessa's birth, and Kiergan had always had a soft spot for their sister.

Who might've usually appreciated that fact, but this time, she just rolled her eyes and nudged his shoulder as she pulled her embroidery from her bag. "I am no' heartbroken, as well ye ken. I'd never even *met* the man."

Nessa's third betrothal had ended yesterday with news of the man's death.

Again.

Finn had met Henry Campbell once, at Scone, and spoke up now. "Mayhap, but he was a good man, as far as I could tell."

His sister just scowled and bent over her stitching. "I might be mourning him harder had I met and approved of our betrothal."

"Dinnae fash, lass," Da boomed out. "We'll have ye betrothed again in nae time. I've heard good things about the Duffus laird's son. His name is Henry, too!"

Nessa might've muttered something like, "Oh, joy," but 'twas hard to tell, because their father lifted his flagon happily at the same moment and announced, "And any sadness *I* might've felt has been erased by the knowledge Finn is ready to accept my terms."

Nudging Finn, Duncan asked, "Ye're really going to marry her?"

"As soon as possible," Finn told his twin with a grin. "Assuming she'll have me."

"With the marriage portion I plan on granting ye lads, her brother'll no' say nay," Da assured him. "There's five of ye who'll no' become laird. What do ye want from me?"

"Naught," Kiergan was quick to assure him, while Rocque looked thoughtful.

"I could be happy as I am. A cottage, mayhap, and my place as Commander."

Finn nodded, knowing the Oliphants were better off with Rocque close by, to watch over the training of the men and command the warriors as need be.

But Finn…?

"The MacIans are no' a large clan," he began thoughtfully, "and their laird has already married off three sisters. He's told Fiona he'd happily sell her and her sister for a hundred head of cattle."

Duncan grunted. "Sounds like real prizes."

Fiona *was* a prize, and although he'd never met her sister, Skye, Finn knew they were close. "My point is, if I could approach him with a bride price and a plan for the future, he'd no' object to our marriage."

It had been that *price* which had stayed his hand all these months. That, and the fact he hadn't had an excuse to travel to MacIan land, or even to Wick. But he'd written her a dozen times over the long winter, and now it was warm enough to embark on trading journeys again, Finn had every intention of making a deal with her brother to take Fiona as his wife.

Da was obviously considering his earlier words, because now he hummed. "I cannae let ye go, laddie, and I hope ye'll understand. No' for a while, at least."

"Go? Cannae let me *go* where?" Finn asked with a frown.

"*Anywhere.* Ye're the Oliphants' best hope in trade. Ye have a silver tongue, lad, and we *need* ye. Ye're the one who gets us the best deals at market and with merchants."

Finn relaxed slightly, realizing his father wasn't forbidding him to go to MacIan territory. "Aye?"

"So ye—and yer wife—will have a place here at Oliphant Castle for as long as ye'd like. Once ye're married, I'll give ye one of the rooms upstairs, and ye can fill the nursery with my grandbairns."

Finn had to grin at that image. "Even if I'm no' laird?"

"Ach, I dinnae mind granddaughters too."

"I cannae believe ye're seriously considering this," Duncan muttered.

Finn lifted one brow at his brother. "Just because *ye* have nae interest in marriage, doesnae mean *I* cannae."

" 'Tis no' the marriage I'm objecting to, but the *bairns*."

Finn's grin grew. He and Duncan were identical in every way, until it came to their personalities. While Finn had always been optimistic and charming—which is what made him so damn good at finding the best bargains for their clan—Duncan was serious and intent, forever focused on perfecting his craft.

"Ye'll make my bairns a fine uncle, Dunc."

"Dinnae call me that." Duncan's habitual response was accompanied by a scowl, but there was a glint in his dark eyes which Finn knew to be humor.

"Aye, Uncle Dunc," he drawled.

In response, his twin hauled back and shoved him, hard enough to slam him into Rocque, who merely grunted. Reaching around Finn, who was now rubbing his sore shoulder, Rocque grabbed Duncan's ale flagon and upended it into the man's lap.

Duncan stood with a curse, then reached across Finn, intent on grabbing the big man. But Da's command stopped him.

"Enough, ye two! Ye'd be better served spending yer time thinking about yer *own* futures."

"Oh, God's Teeth, Da!" The newcomer, Alistair, groaned as he approached the table. "Ye're no' serious about this ridiculous marriage plan, are ye?"

Of all the brothers, Finn would've thought Alistair would be the most impressed with Da's suggestion. He was the one who practically kept the clan going, after all.

Apparently, Da was surprised by Alistair's comment too. "Aye, lad, I am. If ye'd stayed last night, ye would've learned that."

Crossing his arms in front of his chest and leaning one hip against the wall, Alistair rolled his eyes. "I had to finish yer correspondence. And the crop rotation charts were no' going to make themselves."

Kiergan propped his chin up on one fist. "Well, ye missed the best part: Malcolm explaining how to woo a woman, and Finn going on about his lady love."

One of Alistair's brows twitched. "The fair Fiona will finally be part of our family, eh? Lord kens we've spent all winter listening to him pining for her."

Finn sighed. "I've no' been that bad."

"Aye, brother," Alistair intoned solemnly, nodding, "ye have."

Scooping up Duncan's empty flagon—his twin was still standing beside him, dripping—Finn hurled it at their smug brother.

Alistair—damn him—easily ducked out of the way, then turned his attention blandly to their sister. "And how are ye doing this morn, Nessa? Nae tears I see."

She stabbed at her embroidery. "I am fine. I did no' *ken* Henry Campbell. Nor Henry of Elgin, nor Henry Ruthven before him. Da keeps making these betrothals without my blessing."

"Because yer father kens best," Da called out from the other end of the table, while spooning porridge into his mouth.

Obviously trying to distract her, Kiergan nudged her shoulder again. "What are ye working on this time?" He craned his head to see her embroidery. "Is that a battle ax?"

"Nay." She pointed one slim finger at her design, although Finn couldn't see it. " 'Tis a great sword. *That* is the battle ax."

"Ah, and that's a severed head, complete with little drops of blood," Kiergan murmured weakly, straightening. "How clever."

For the first time, Nessa smiled, a fierce sort of smile, as she stared down at her work. "Aye. 'Twill be lovely when complete."

Swallowing, Kiergan met Finn's gaze, and Finn did his best not to laugh at his brother's discomfort. Wee Nessa had grown into a woman over the last few years, and she now had a mind of her own.

How could she not, being raised with six older brothers?

Despite their efforts to turn the conversation, Da was like a dog with a bone. "Alistair, lad! Are ye saying ye're against my scheme?"

Alistair dropped his chin with a sigh. "I'm *saying* that I dinnae have time for yer scheme, Da. Find a woman to marry me? Before yer deadline? Do ye no' realize how much work I have to do here?"

"Aye." Da was nodding. "Remember, *I* used to do it all before ye got too big for yer kilt." Ignoring for Rocque's predictable chuckle, Da shook his head. "I want ye to take the time to *find* a lass to marry ye. *Make* time."

"Kiergan, can ye no' do it?" Alistair snapped to his twin.

Kiergan reared back. "Marry ye? Nay!"

"*Find* me a woman to marry. Do it by proxy! I care no'!"

Duncan leaned forward. "Surely ye could spare a lass or two, Kiergan, from the many always following ye around, swooning?"

Before Kiergan could retort—likely something rude, judging from his gesture—Da slammed his bowl down on the table.

"I am still the laird around here, lads!" he roared. "If I say ye'll be married and start presenting me with grandbairns, then 'tis as good as done." With a growl, he pushed back from the table and stood, piercing each of them with a glare. "Ye best think long and hard on what kind of lass ye want as a wife, because ye're no' getting out of this. For the good of the clan, I *must* pick an heir, and with all of ye being so close in age, this is the fairest method. I love ye all—although I dinnae say it enough—and I want what's best for ye."

"*Marriage*," groaned Duncan.

"Aye, *marriage*. 'Tis no' so horrible as ye think."

Rocque was the one to say what they were all thinking. "So how come ye never remarried after losing Nessa's mother?"

Da's face slowly turned red above his beard. "Because!" he roared. "*Because* I had six strapping sons, and *my* father wasnae alive to tell me my duty!"

Finn hid his smile as his brothers shifted uncomfortably or muttered in irritation. "I dinnae mind yer scheme, Da."

"Suck up," Duncan murmured, at the same time Kiergan hurled a piece of bread at Finn's head, causing his smile to grow even as he ducked.

But it had worked.

Da's breathing had calmed, and his coloring was returning to normal.

Finally, he grunted and nodded to Finn. "Send a letter to Laird MacLan today, inviting him and his lovely sisters to visit. We'll have ye married before the fortnight is out, lad."

While Finn doubted miracles could be achieved so quickly, he was ready to try. Leaning forward, he caught Malcolm's eye. "Ye'll write it for me?"

Although he could read and write as well as any of his brothers, he preferred working with numbers. But there was another reason.

"Malcolm's got the neatest hand of any of us," Alistair offered. "Laird MacLan will appreciate that."

When Finn nodded in agreement, Rocque chuckled. "Have him add the little flourishes and curlicues he does. Lasses like that."

As Malcolm agreed, Kiergan rolled his eyes. "Ye lot really have *nae* idea how to woo a woman, do ye?"

Finn's grin grew. "I have nae need to woo this lass. We hold each other's hearts already."

With his father's blessing, and the promise of a future here with the clan, he had something tangible to offer Fiona. He thought of her letters, the ones he kept in a small chest and removed to read when he missed her. Even though he fully believed she loved him too, he wouldn't know for certain until she arrived.

Until she arrived at Oliphant Castle, and he offered for her.

Then he'd know if he had a chance at a future with Fiona MacLan.

CHAPTER 2

IT TOOK three days to reach the Oliphant holding north of the Gunns, and Fiona thought she'd go mad with impatience.

Soon. Soon, she kept whispering to herself.

Soon she'd see Finn again.

Would he still make her heart flutter, the way he had when she'd met him?

Would his touch still make her warm all over, and the look in his eyes still cause her inner muscles to clench?

Would she still go breathless with anticipation around him, wondering if he would kiss her?

Would he kiss her?

"Of course, ye ninny, he wants to *marry* ye."

Riding beside her, on her magnificent gray gelding, Skye clucked her tongue. "Ye're talking to yerself again."

Fiona sent her twin sister—*identical* twin sister—a chagrined glance. "Sorry."

"Dinnae fash. Ye're thinking of Finn again, aye?"

Mayhap she *shouldn't* be. Any time she thought of Finn, she thought of Finn's *kisses*, and the fire he'd lit inside her. She thought of how he'd touched her, how he'd stroked her skin and made her moan, and *that* caused her to shift a little in the saddle.

Skye must've seen it, because she made a little noise halfway between a snort and a laugh, but didn't draw any more attention to Fiona's discomfort.

But her sister would know of it. They'd shared a room their entire life and had giggled and chattered on about the way a fine-looking shoulder, or a well-muscled chest, could make them feel. And after Fiona had met Finn at Wick, she'd told her sister all about the *feelings* he'd brought out in her.

And Skye had known her well enough to find excuses to leave the room when Fiona needed to relieve some of those feelings with her own fingers.

Just thinking of those releases made her cheeks warm, and she tilted her head back to catch the sunshine, afraid someone might guess what she was thinking.

As always, Skye understood. "Ye best hope Stewart's men think that's just the sun causing those flushes."

"I dinnae— *Bah!*" Fiona made a rude gesture, dismissing her sister's teasing.

"And ye should *definitely* hope they dinnae guess ye understood what *that* means."

"*Skye!*"

Chuckling, her twin turned her attention back to the road in front of them. Stewart rode ahead with about half of his guard. Fiona assumed they were speaking of manly things such as swords and farting, and whether a woman's tits or arse were more appealing.

On the road behind the sisters, another half-dozen MacIan warriors rode, although these men were younger and among those she and Skye used to spy upon when they bathed in the river.

Not that she had any interest in them *now*, of course. Not when she was on her way to visit *Finn*.

"Do ye think we'll be to Oliphant Castle in time for the evening meal as Stewart said?" she asked her sister.

Skye glanced upward, as if judging the weather on this fine morning. She was somewhat of an expert on traveling distances via horse, although their older brother—nor many others—had any inkling. "Aye, nae reason no' to. We havenae dallied, and yer love doesnae live so verra far away from home."

"I'm glad," Fiona said quietly. " 'Twill mean I'm able to see ye, if this marriage happens."

"*When* this marriage happens, ye mean," her twin corrected, shooting her a smirk. "If ye think I've sent my men into hiding for a fortnight, and ridden all this way with ye, just for the man to turn coward, ye're wrong. If he doesnae sign the contract, yer Finn will do it with my blade to his back!"

The thought of Finn being forced to do *anything* made Fiona smile. "He included a letter to me with his letter to Stewart, although this one was in his own hand." After the long winter's worth of letters from him, she recognized his writing. "Did I show it to ye?"

"Aye, along with the other dozen or so." Skye jerked her chin to the leather satchel hanging from Fiona's saddle. "Even now, they're no' far from ye, are they?"

Instinctually, Fiona's hand dropped to her precious collection of letters. "Nay," she murmured happily, knowing her twin was right. She'd read and re-read Finn's letters more times than she could count. "I'll keep them for our children to read."

"*All* of them?"

Skye's knowing tone had Fiona stifling her giggle. "Mayhap no' *all* of them." A few had been rather…descriptive.

"Good. The future Oliphant doesnae need to ken that sort of thing about his parents," her sister quipped with a wink.

The Oliphant.

Although Finn's formal letter to Laird Stewart MacIan—which Fiona was certain had been written by someone else, judging from all the curlicues and flourishes—had mentioned only a marriage alliance, his personal letter to her had told much more.

He'd been open about his father's declaration. William Oliphant had declared the first of his sons to present him with a legitimate grandson would become the next laird, and that grandson after him. 'Twas a bit daunting to know she *might* become the lady of a large clan…but not until at least nine months after her marriage.

That thought led to another, and soon she was flushed again, thinking of Finn's kisses.

His kisses…and more.

"I ken that look," Skye murmured drily. "Ye're thinking of Finn again, are ye no'?"

Fiona's fingers were still caressing the satchel with the letters. "He told me he was looking forward to our wedding with joy."

"The *wedding*?" Skye chuckled wryly. "From what ye told me of the two of ye, he's looking forward to the *bedding*."

Fiona's smile grew at the jest, knowing it was true. "Me too," she confessed, which sent both lasses into chuckles.

Ahead, their oldest brother and laird of their small clan turned to frown at them. The twins both snapped their spines straight and sent Stewart pleasant, if vacuous, smiles. He was a man who was focused on propriety and image, and wanted his sisters to be as well.

Which would be difficult, considering their…*hobbies*.

Eventually, Stewart nodded, obviously pleased with their attempts to resemble proper young ladies, and turned back to his men and the route ahead.

As Skye let out a sigh and slumped into a more comfortable position, Fiona patted her headdress. She hated the elaborate netting and much preferred her sister's simple braid, but Stewart had given her an earful about looking her best to meet her betrothed's family.

Of course, if she had her druthers, she and Finn wouldn't be thinking about clothing at *all*.

"He's gotten to be a real pain," Skye muttered, glaring daggers at their brother's back. "Since he married Allison, he walks around with a stick up his arse."

Fiona hummed. "That must make walking difficult."

"Aye. Imagine how uncomfortable *riding* must be," her twin

agreed wryly. "But Allison likes him like that, and I wish the two of them all the luck in the world, since they deserve one another."

"If I marry Finn, I'll miss ye and Nurse, but I'll *no'* miss Allison. She's made life...difficult. At home, I mean."

"Difficult? She's made life bloody impossible. Do ye ken Stewart actually took me to task for that gown I commissioned last Yule? He said the velvet train was too costly." Skye spat out a curse. "As if *I* wanted to wear a bloody gown *or* a bloody train! *He* was the one who—"

"Aye, I ken it," Fiona interrupted. "Allison told him we needed to appear as sisters of a great man, remember? She was the one who commissioned the damnable things, with nae thought to the amount of material they would take."

"Or what that material would cost." Skye's lips curled upward from their habitual scowl. "Which wasnae as much as it should've, thanks to ye."

Fiona inclined her head, acknowledging the compliment. Since her brother's marriage to a woman who saw no need to conserve the clan's meager funds, she'd taken it upon herself to do much of the trading.

When merchants didn't stop by the MacIan lands, she went to them, or to market centers like Wick.

Where she'd haggled for that bolt of green velvet and had met the most perfectly handsome dark-eyed charmer.

"But as I recall," she reminded her sister, "we would no' have even had the coin for that purchase—or Allison's other demands—without yer help."

"Help?" Skye shook her head and adjusted her position on her finely tooled leather saddle—which she claimed had been a gift, but Fiona knew the truth. " 'Twas no' *my* help, but the generosity of the Bishop when I met him the fortnight before on the road to Inverness."

"The blessed Father provided for us, did he no'?"

Without missing a beat, Skye shrugged. "God helps those who help themselves."

Lifting her fingertips to her lips to stifle her giggle, Fiona shot her sister a warning glance. It would not do for Stewart to learn where most of the clan's money had come from these last few years.

But then Skye surprised her by sighing. "Ach, Fee. What are we to do without ye?"

"Without my haggling?"

"Without *ye*." Skye's fingers tightened around the reins of her favorite mount. "Life at home will be miserable with only Allison as company, now that she's breeding."

The thought of being parted from her twin did indeed bring tears to Fiona's eyes, but she reminded herself they'd known this day was coming. Although Skye had shown no interest in marriage, Fiona had always known she'd one day have to leave her sister to start her own life.

And since meeting Finn, she'd been preparing—half-hoping, half-dreading—for that moment.

So she cleared her throat. "She *has* gotten more demanding, has she no'? Luckily, she has months to go, or Stewart would no' have considered leaving her side to accompany me. *Us*." She swallowed, trying to focus on a bright part. "I'll miss the bairn. I would love to meet our niece or nephew. Ye're lucky ye'll get to hold him."

"Or *her*," Skye quickly corrected. "Or *them*. Have ye ever considered she might have twins?"

The sisters met each other's gaze, identical blue eyes twinkling.

"God help her if they're aught like us," Fiona said in a serious tone, knowing Skye was struggling not to smile.

"Here's something else to consider," her sister pointed out, with a raised brow. "What if the two of ye have twins?"

Bairns.

Unconsciously, Fiona's hand dropped from her lips to her stomach.

Finn's bairns.

Twins?

Was that a possibility?

The thought terrified her as much as it made her heart tighten with excitement.

"Fee?" her sister asked quietly. "Ye look as if ye've seen a ghost."

"Ghosts are no' real," Fiona snapped quickly, the old debate easy to fall back into. "Ye ken that."

Rather than obliging her, Skye just shrugged. "Fine then. Ye look the way ye looked when, three years ago, I dared ye to spend the whole day in the lambing sheds, and ye saw that ewe birth a lamb with two heads, and I convinced ye 'twas a sign of the Devil. Remember all the mucus and blood and shite...and *mucus*?"

God's Wounds, why did her sister keep coming back to the mucus?

The disgusting reminder had Fiona pressing her hand against her stomach again, but for another reason this time. "I didnae eat mutton for months after."

"Ye *still* dinnae care for the smell of it, and aye, that look." When Fiona glanced at her sister, Skye nodded unhelpfully. "That one right there. Ye look as if ye're going to be sick. Because I brought up Finn's bairns? Do ye no' want any? Or was it the two-headed lamb, which—"

"By all the saints, Skye, would ye shut up about the two-headed lamb!" Fiona hissed, swallowing down the sour taste in her throat, as she turned back to the road and settled herself more comfortably in the stupid *lady's saddle* her brother insisted she use. "Nay, 'tis nae the idea of bairns which bothered me," she confessed.

Skye couldn't let more than a minute pass, before clearing her throat. "Well? What is it then?"

Fiona sighed. She'd spent months thinking of Finn, imagining him touching her the way he'd promised, imagined spending a lifetime with him.

But what if...?

"What if he's no' as wonderful as I remember?" she whispered.

Her sister's response was immediate. "He is. I ken it."

When Fiona snuck a glance, Skye nodded firmly.

"The two of ye have a love I'd no' expected to see in person, and ye're lucky to be able to marry, assuming Stewart is satisfied with the bride price. Finn Oliphant is a fine man. Handsome, charming, funny, and smart ye said. He has no' changed."

Fiona swallowed, unable to meet her sister's eyes. Instead, she stared at one of her palfrey's ears as the animal picked its way delicately along the rutted road.

"What if *I* have changed?" she finally whispered.

"What?"

"What if he nae longer feels the way he used to about me? What if...what if another has caught his eye? I ken I'm nae great beauty. I dinnae want to marry a man who—"

"First of all, if ye're nae great beauty, then neither am I," her sister began in a hard voice. "And were we no' atop horses, I'd pull yer hair for that insult."

Before Fiona's lips could do more than twitch, Skye continued.

"And *third* of all, why in *damnation* would he propose a betrothal, if he was planning on dallying with another? He wants to marry ye, Fiona, same as he told ye last autumn, same as all his letters have stated."

Logically, she knew this. But there was a part of her, a part which looked at Allison and their older sisters and saw great courtly beauty, which told Fiona she was nothing special.

So why did Finn seem to think she was?

She sighed. "Second?"

"Second what?" Skye snapped.

"*Second* of all? Ye skipped second."

"Fine. *Second of all*, ye're a damnable fool for worrying about something like this, when yer heart and mind ken 'tis nae true."

"I ken ax-wielding ghosts are no' true, but I still worry about them."

"Aye, well, sometimes ye're verra weak-minded, Fee."

Bantering with her sister made her heart lighter, her worry less. Fiona nodded solemnly. "If ye call me crazed, I can call ye ugly."

"If ye call me ugly," her identical twin sister pointed out, "then ye'll make *me* crazed."

Fiona raised herself in her saddle and made a point of looking at the men riding with their brother ahead of them, before twisting to study the warriors behind.

Then she settled back and smiled brightly at her sister.

"I can say, with absolute certainty, we are the prettiest MacIans on the road today."

Their laughter earned them another glared reprimand from Stewart, but it was worth it.

As Skye had predicted, the MacIan party arrived at the Oliphant keep mid-afternoon. Both sisters craned their heads back to stare up at the grand edifice as they rode through the outer gate, while Stewart attempted to appear blasé and accustomed to such splendor.

Truthfully, Oliphant Castle was not the most magnificent holding she'd ever seen; why, once Fiona had been as far as Scone on her trading journeys! But this was the most magnificent one she'd ever been *invited inside*.

And if things really did work out between her and Finn, she'd be *living* there.

Assuming he still wanted her.

Then they were through the inner gate, and their men spread out around them. Beside her, Skye whistled under her breath.

"Is that him?"

When Fiona glanced her way, her twin nodded to the main doors of the keep.

Fiona turned back…and caught her breath.

Oliphant Castle was magnificent, aye, but not nearly as magnificent as the man striding toward them, an easy grin on his gorgeous face, his hand raised in greeting.

Finn was even more handsome than she remembered.

His light hair was long enough he wore two braids down his temples, to hold it out of his eyes, and his dark blue eyes sparkled with a merriment which matched his smile. When he saw her and Skye seated atop their horses, his smile grew even larger, and his pace increased.

Time seemed to slow for Fiona as he crossed the courtyard. Each stride appeared to be in slow-motion; his kilt slowly bouncing against his muscular thighs, as the breeze lifted his long locks. Fiona swore she heard music building to a romantic crescendo, matching the frantic tempo of her heart, as he tilted his head back. The sun glinted off his teeth in a way which made no sound, but *should've* sounded like a *"gling"*.

Good God, mayhap I have *gone crazed.*

Before she could wonder at her own imagination, time suddenly sped up to normal speed as Finn finally reached them, and she opened her mouth to call his name….

…And then choked on her own tongue when, with a gallant call of, "My darling!" her love reached up and swept *her sister* off her horse!

Before Skye could utter more than "Erp?," Finn had spun her around in a circle, with that damnable romantic music pounding in the back of Fiona's mind making a mockery of the whole cock-up.

She cleared her throat pointedly.

Apparently not hearing her, Finn was smiling as he took his time to lower Skye to her feet. If Fiona's sound of disapproval didn't clue him in to the issue, the way her twin was glaring at him might.

Still seated atop her palfrey, Fiona watched Finn's brows draw in as he stared at Skye's furious expression.

"Fee—" he began, right before Skye hauled off and punched him in the shoulder.

Before her sister might say something which would offend the watching Oliphants, Fiona cleared her throat again. More pointedly. *Sword-tip* pointedly. And added a, "Ahem?" for good measure.

It worked.

Finn's attention swung to her, and she saw the exact moment he understood what had happened. First his expression went slack, then amusement began to dawn in those lovely dark eyes of his.

"Twins?" His head swiveled back and forth between Fiona and Skye. "God's tits, ye're *twins*?"

Before either of them could speak, he stepped away from Skye, chuckling. "I should've kenned my sweet Fiona wouldnae hurt me." He approached her palfrey, arms raised to lift her down. "And I kenned ye wouldnae frown at me so."

In the face of his smile, her concern eased, and as he'd intended, she smiled. "Ye are such a charmer, my Finn. But I do understand the confusion. Skye and I *are* identical, and 'tis sorry I am I never told ye so."

"Identical?" He laughed, reaching her with outstretched arms. "Aye, I ken all about that. And on another note, I like the sound of '*My Finn*' on yer lips. Would ye like to try this again?"

Smiling, she leaned sideways, trusting him to catch her, and she wasn't disappointed.

His strong hands wrapped around her waist, and she reveled in the way he lifted her easily, spinning her in a circle as he lifted her down. She went a little light-headed, as the last moments repeated themselves. The swoop, the spin, the odd music playing in her mind, *everything*.

And this time, it was perfect.

She sighed as her toes touched the ground, and his arms snaked around her back. With her hands on his shoulders, she smiled up at him.

"My Finn," she whispered happily.

"My Fiona."

That sounded lovely, didn't it?

Fiona wondered what—

And then she wasn't thinking at all, as his lips claimed hers.

Right there in Oliphant Castle's courtyard, he kissed her, before God and his relatives and Stewart and his men, and Fiona didn't care. She wrapped her arms around his neck and didn't bother swallowing down her moan.

Remembering what he'd taught her when it came to the art of kissing, she brushed her tongue along the seam of his lips and was rewarded with him tightening his hold on her, causing her pelvis to press against the hardness under his kilt.

The sensation made her throb—made her entire *body* throb, which she hadn't thought possible—with longing, and she resisted the urge to wriggle against him. Then his tongue was in her mouth and—*Holy Mother*—did it feel good!

It was several long moments later before she realized she was bent backward, his arms the only thing holding her up, her fingers playing in his hair.

Slowly, he pulled her lower lip between his teeth, and she moaned in pleasure as she reluctantly came back to herself and the present.

That throbbing is damnably distracting.

Someone was clearing his throat. It wasn't Finn, because Finn was still holding her, bent forward, smiling down into her eyes and feeling so *perfect*, she still couldn't seem to draw a full breath.

"Ahem."

Blast. There it was again.

Sounded like Stewart, damn him.

Finn must've maintained more of his senses than she did, because his grin turned wry as he straightened, pulling her upright. Fiona wasn't sure she could stand on her own, but luckily, she didn't have to.

He still hadn't released her, and my it felt good.

And the look in his eyes—the *promise* in his eyes—felt even better.

"Ahem!"

Definitely Stewart.

Still smiling, still not releasing her, Finn turned to address her brother. "Welcome to Oliphant Castle, my friends. Do join us inside. My father and his housekeeper have been planning a grand feast for tonight to celebrate yer arrival." His arm tightened around her waist. "And we can discuss business."

Then he glanced back down at her and winked. "And by business, I mean our betrothal."

Her knees were weak. Her heart was thumping frantically. She couldn't catch her breath, and her core—her tight inner muscles—was still throbbing.

"Still a charmer," she whispered, smiling in anticipation.

"Always, my love."

CHAPTER 3

FINN WAS STUCK SITTING beside Rocque to his left, with Aunt Agatha just on the other side of his brother, which Finn was certain was on purpose.

Oh, not that he disliked this brother of his, or normally minded the daft old bat. Aunt Agatha was a delight to get rambling, and just sit and nurse a mug of ale and *listen* to. Especially her stories about growing up at Oliphant Castle, two generations before. She was actually Da's aunt, their great aunt.

But tonight she was in rare form, entertaining everyone around her with tales of Da's childhood exploits. Thank God *he* was sitting farther down the table, several seats to Finn's right, entertaining Stewart MacIan, and couldn't hear her description of his naked arse the time he lost the bet with the shepherd's sons on who could piss the farthest.

William Oliphant had won, of course.

While Rocque roared with laughter, Finn turned away from that little group to the woman directly to his right.

"I'm sorry ye have to hear all of this," he murmured, covering Fiona's hand, where it rested beside their shared trencher.

Blushing prettily, she sent him a glance from under her lashes. "I'm no'. I think yer family is delightful."

At the sight of her flush, Finn felt his chest go tight, and all his blood rush southward. He swallowed, wondering if there was any way he could sneak her off alone.

By St. Ninian's ankles, he needed to be alone with her!

It had been too long since he'd had her in his arms, and had her brother not interrupted them this afternoon in the courtyard, Finn wondered how far he might've gone. He'd been only moments away from groping her, from untying her gown and shoving his hand inside to squeeze her small breasts, the way he'd been dreaming of doing all winter.

Down, lad, he thought to his cock.

It did no good.

Having her in his arms again—for such a short amount of time— had been bliss and torture all at once.

And had only whetted his appetite for more.

For now though, they were surrounded by his family, and hers. So he just squeezed her fingers and tried to convey all his longing in his tone, when he said, "I'm glad ye think so, for they will soon be yer family."

Across the table, her sister—her *identical twin sister*—made a noise very much like a snort. Skye MacIan still hadn't forgiven him for embracing her, thinking she was Fiona. But 'twas an honest mistake, and Finn felt no shame nor embarrassment over it.

So he sent his soon-to-be-sister-in-law a charming smile. "Ye dinnae agree?"

Skye was slouched in her chair, her arms folded across her chest, ignoring Kiergan's attempts—who was sitting beside her—to flirt with her. Instead, she'd been sending glares at *Finn*.

Now she sat forward, her gaze locked on their joined hands. "I think yer family is likely as wild and uncouth as *ye* are."

"*Skye!*" Fiona gasped in astonishment.

But Finn squeezed her hand. "Nay, yer sister is right, my love." He inclined his head to the woman across from him. "Ye have my apologies, Lady Skye, for placing my hands on yer person so inappropriately. I kenned my Fiona had a sister, and mayhap I kenned she was a twin…but I had nae idea ye were identical. I should've kenned that."

While Fiona murmured, " 'Twas my fault for no' mentioning it," Skye harrumphed and sat back in her chair.

Finally, she blew out a breath. "*Well.* At least ye apologize prettily. I forgive ye." To his surprise, the look she shot Fiona was tinged with a hint of concern. "As long as ye dinnae make a habit out of embracing other women when my sister is around. Or *no'* around for that matter."

Chuckling, Finn lifted Fiona's hand to his lips and brushed a kiss across her fingers. "Despite my earlier gaffe, ye must believe me when I say I have nae intention of ever looking at another woman, as long as Fiona is mine."

Fiona sighed happily, Skye nodded firmly, and Stewart—who was on Fiona's other side—leaned over. "Well, I think yer family is charming. Despite the lack of manners some of them display"—his eyes cut toward Finn's brothers, although it was impossible to tell which ones—"a few of them are delightful."

With raised brows, Finn murmured a noncommittal "Oh?"

From what Fiona had told him about Stewart, he hadn't expected the man to *like* his family, any of them.

He'd considered instructing his family to be on their best behavior to try to impress the man, but knew it would have been a lost cause. They were all uncouth, untamed, and wildly *fun*.

But now Stewart sent a grin across the table to Finn's sister, Nessa. "Aye, there are a *few* Oliphants I wouldnae mind kenning further. If I were no' married already, I would ask yer father to consider a connection to yer lovely sister."

On the other side of the table, next to Nessa, Kiergan stifled a belch as he reached for his flagon. "Da would say nay. Nae offense, being a laird and all"—he paused to take a swig—"but ye're no' named Henry, and Da has a system."

Before Stewart could ask what he meant, Finn's brothers who were near enough to overhear burst into laughter at the jest. Nessa had only been betrothed thrice, but all of them had been named

Henry, and her brothers had great fun in teasing her about the un-necessity of remembering a new name to call in the throes of passion.

Although the idea of *his sister*, engaged in the throes of passion, cooled whatever ardor Finn might've been feeling from holding Fiona's hand in his.

While the others tossed jokes back and forth—mainly at Nessa's expense, although she could certainly hold her own—Fiona pulled him closer.

Aaand…there went his ardor, sky-high once more.

"Kiergan is the one next to my sister, aye?" she murmured. When he nodded, she continued, "And Rocque is beside yer aunt, with Malcolm the quiet one across from him?"

"Aye," he murmured in response, glad for the excuse to put his head near hers. "Although he's no' usually this quiet. He must be thinking about something. Remind me to tell ye of his new idea for a beard-trimmer."

Her lips tugged upward. "And Alistair is the brother seated next to Malcolm, aye?" When he nodded again, she continued, "So where is the sixth brother? Ye told me the two of ye shared a mother."

"Oh, aye, Duncan." Finn straightened, but propped his elbow on the table so he was still facing her when he explained. "He's taken after our stepfather as a smith, although he works with precious metals. His Master lives in Larg, and has called for him. He was preparing to leave this afternoon, but I confess I was excited about yer arrival, I dinnae ken if he left afore or after yer party reached Oliphant Castle."

"Is he normally here, or in Larg?"

Finn smiled fondly. "Here. He and I technically share a room, but years ago he set up a cot down in the forge where our stepfather works and has lived there ever since."

Her eyes lit up. "Ye have *more* family nearby?"

By St. Ninian's blessed armpits, her smile was lovely!

Fiona MacIan was not the *most* beautiful woman he'd ever seen —even Nessa, with her habitual scowls, had more pleasing features

—but when Fiona smiled, she was *perfect*. It had been her wit, her intelligence, her kindness, and her grace which had attracted him originally, but the longer he sat beside her, the more her beauty showed.

"Aye," he managed to croak out past a dry throat. Swallowing, he tried again, and reminded his cock to stay where it was. "Aye, our mother lives in the village, married, with a few bairns. I'll introduce ye, if ye'd like."

"Oh, Finn!" Her smile grew as her fingers tightened around his. "If we are to be married, they will be my family as well. I'd like verra much to ken them."

He nodded firmly, liking the idea of the two of them having a future with his large, rambling family. "I'll take ye to visit them tomorrow."

"Break it up, ye two lovebirds!"

Startled, Finn jerked back, just in time for Brohn to reach across the table between Skye and Malcolm and plop a new flagon of ale down. When Finn scowled at him, Brohn just winked back. "We cannae have ye mooning all over one another for the *entire* meal. Ye're putting the rest of us off our beef!"

"What in damnation is a lovebird?" Finn growled with a shake of his head.

But Brohn had already moved on, delivering more ale to the laird. Shrugging, Skye reached for the flagon. "Birds who are in love?"

"That's ridiculous!" Fiona giggled.

"Why?" Rocque called from Finn's other side. "We say that the dog is loyal to his master, and the bull is proud. Why can birds no' be in love?"

Finn clapped his brother on the shoulder. "That is surprisingly romantic, coming from ye."

The big man's cheerful smile flashed. "Aye, and I'll break yer arm if ye hit me again."

As Finn ruffled Rocque's hair, and the bigger man ducked out of the way, cursing, Malcolm smiled. " 'Tis common enough to attribute anthropomorphic characteristics to animals, and Brohn was merely—"

"Ampomothac? God's tits, he's speaking in tongues again," Kiergan groaned.

As the table—at least, those who heard the curse—chuckled, Lara stepped up between Skye and Kiergan, holding a tray of tarts. "Sweets, anyone?"

Kiergan snapped upright, his easy scowl melting. "Ye shouldnae be working. Ye should celebrate with us." He took the tray from her and set it in front of Stewart, then scooched over. "Here, sit down."

With only a little hesitation—and a shy smile—the pretty young woman squeezed herself onto the bench and accepted a tart from Kiergan; a happy blush upon her face.

"This is Lara," Finn explained to Fiona. "She's Moira's—the housekeeper's—daughter. She and her brother, Brohn"—he pointed at the man still delivering ale to the revelers—"were raised with all of us. Lara, this is Fiona MacIan." He lifted Fiona's hand to his lips again, and with a reverent tone, said, "My *betrothed*."

And the way Fiona smiled in return made him go rock-hard under his kilt.

From two seats down, on his other side, Aunt Agatha piped up again. "Ye're no' officially betrothed yet, laddie. Those papers have to be signed before ye can make the drummer happy!"

"Drummer?" Fiona asked, as her sister's brows went up.

"Ach, aye!"

Agatha leaned forward, her plump face drawn into a rictus of a smile. It was her ghost-story-telling face, and Finn noticed he wasn't the only one of his brothers rolling his eyes.

"The Ghostly Drummer of Oliphant Castle. Ye've no' heard of him?" the old woman asked.

When the MacIan sisters shook their heads, she cackled gleefully.

"Ask these laddies. They've been hearing him oft of late, especially since Wee Willie came up with this scheme of his."

Leave it to Agatha to refer to Laird William Oliphant as "Wee Willie."

Skye was frowning. "A ghost? Who— What? His presence portends something?"

Malcolm sighed. "Other castles have spirits, remainders of the past. Some wail, some shriek, some cry, some warn of doom."

"Ours plays the drum," his twin said with a nod.

" 'Tis verra annoying," Kiergan muttered.

"Ours warns of doom! *Doom!*" Aunt Agatha cried, her hands flapping above her head in emphasis. "*Doom!*"

Fiona pulled her hand from his, and when he turned in concern, he found she was holding both in front of her lips.

In fear?

Her lovely blue eyes were wide, but he couldn't tell if it was humor or terror shining from within them.

" 'Tis naught to be concerned with, Fee," he began.

"But ye've heard the drumming?" she asked. "*All* of ye?"

Finn shifted in his seat, not sure he wanted to tell her all of it. "I heard it last year. Dunc was complaining of it just recently."

"Oh dear," she whispered. "We have a ghost at MacIan Castle. She's friendly. Warns us when the cheese is going to turn. No' that I believe in her, of course."

"If ye did," her sister pointed out, "ye might no' have eaten that spoiled cheese at Hogmany."

Fiona ignored her. "But if both of ye have heard this ghostly drummer—"

"*Dooooooom!*" Agatha shrieked.

Rocque snorted. "I dinnae see the big deal. *I* can barely sleep for all the damned drumming."

Well *that* shut everyone right up.

"Ye've heard it too?" Malcolm asked incredulously, just as Finn clarified, "Ye're certain?"

Their brother shrugged. "Sure. I've been hearing it for at least a year, which I thought was bloody strange, seeing as how I dinnae sleep in the keep much these days."

Finn met Kiergan's eyes, and as one, they turned to Malcolm—who shrugged, as if to say he wasn't sure why Rocque would be hallucinating, and mayhap they shouldn't tease him.

"*Doooooooooooooooooooooommmmmmm!*"

"Oh, come off it, Aunt Agatha," Kiergan mumbled.

"A toast!"

Finn wasn't sure who the first one to call out the words had been, but soon, most of the clan was slamming their cups against the table and calling out. He saw Malcolm blow out a breath and glance toward the ceiling as he mouthed, "Thank God," but Kiergan groaned and dropped his head into his hands.

It was Da who stood first, lifting his flagon and turning to Finn. Knowing what was expected of him, Finn draped his arm across the back of Fiona's chair and took her hand in his other. This picture of intimacy garnered some cheers and hoots.

When she blushed, he grinned.

"A toast!" William Oliphant cried, lifting his flagon high. "To the fair Fiona MacIan, who has graced us with her, uh…her grace! And her brother, who will make a strong ally! And to my son, Finn, who is surely my favorite, seeing as how he's about to *finally* make me a grandda!"

God bless her, Nessa reached out and pulled on her father's sleeve. "Oh, sit *down*, ye auld goat."

As the clan erupted into cheers and laughter, Fiona's cheeks turned as pink as her lips, and her fingers tightened around his. But when he met her eyes, worried she might be mortified at Da's talk of procreation, all he saw was anticipation.

Oh.

Had he thought himself rock hard before?

The knowledge *she* wanted him—wanted his bairns—was enough to make him light-headed. Or mayhap that was because his brain was missing most of his blood.

Her tongue darted out, dragging across her lower lip, and Finn couldn't help himself. Damn all these people watching, he *had* to taste her.

He was leaning toward her, ready to capture her lips with his, when his elbow was jostled by Rocque as he stood up.

"To Finn and Fiona! May ye make lots and lots of babies, and become a good laird, so I dinnae have to!"

Finn jerked upright once more, remembering where he was and what was going on, just in time to see Rocque throw back his head and guzzle down all the ale in his flagon, to many cheers from the clan.

Malcolm took that as his cue and stood with his own flagon. "To the fair Fiona, who would make a good Lady Oliphant, assuming Finn can charm his way into her arms!"

This time it was Finn who flushed at the laughter. It was the tightening of Fiona's fingers around his which reminded him she cared for him already, and he clung to that knowledge.

On Malcolm's heels, Kiergan thrust himself to his feet, having forgotten his flagon. When Lara handed it to him with an indulgent smile, he winked down at her and smiled. "Thank ye, love."

Lifting the flagon high, he turned to the clan.

"To my brother, Finn, the bravest among us! The institute of holy matrimony is no' to be trifled with, but he cares naught for rules, and plans to"—he waggled his brows suggestively—"*trifle* as much as possible."

Before the crowd could react, Kiergan thrust his flagon toward Finn, the ale splashing over the side. "To Finn! We're so pleased that unsightly rash of yers cleared up!"

As the great hall erupted into laughter and jeers, Finn surged to his feet to throw himself across the table at his brother. Only their father's words stopped him.

"Come now," Da boomed, slapping Stewart MacIan on the shoulder. "I have the betrothal papers in my solar. Let us read them over."

As Fiona's brother nodded and stood, Da jerked his chin at Alistair. "Come, lad, ye might as well witness this. 'Tis yer hand on the contract, and yer solar these days as much as mine."

Finn's free hand was curled into a fist, ready to break Kiergan's nose, but it was the glare Alistair shot his twin, which halted Kiergan's teasing more than anything. Kiergan might be the prankster of their group, the brother who would never settle down...but none of them could defy Alistair's cold *"behave yerself"* warning.

When Alistair nodded to Finn, telling him to come along, Finn exhaled. Suddenly, Kiergan's jokes didn't seem to matter as much anymore. Not when he was about to look over his *betrothal* contract.

But before he could leave, Fiona tugged on his hand. She'd stood with him when he'd surged to his feet, and now pulled him toward her, so she could whisper in his ear.

"Will ye tell me how it goes?"

Her trust, her willingness to build a life with him, despite not being allowed to sign her own betrothal contract, humbled him.

Quickly, he brushed a kiss against her cheek. "Of course, my love."

Her eyes were twinkling with excitement—and anticipation—when she smiled up at him. "I will leave my door unbarred."

And that, more than anything, had him hurrying to get this betrothal business over with.

CHAPTER 4

SHE AND SKYE had been placed in Finn's room, and wasn't *that* interesting?

Oh, Finn wasn't staying in it, because *propriety*.

But as was common when clans hosted guests, they were put in rooms belonging to members of the household. Alistair had given up his room to Stewart, and Finn's room had gone to the MacIan twins.

Of course, she hadn't realized whose room she and her sister had been placed in initially, but as soon as she and Skye had moved in, Fiona had noticed a sense of familiarity in the items furnishing the room. She'd asked one of the maids and discovered the room belonged to Finn and Duncan, although as Finn had mentioned, Duncan rarely stayed here, preferring his space at the forge.

As Fiona paced and waited for news of her betrothal, her eyes fell on little reminders of Finn, and she was comforted.

Arranged on a shelf beside the window was a ledger and stylus, which contained records of his trades and notes about important reminders, carefully arranged in Finn's hand. She straightened the spare Oliphant plaid which was folded in a small trunk, and inspected the two small swords hung on the wall. Fiona dragged her fingers along the edge of a well-worn table, and wondered if he'd sat here, in the light from the window, and calculated his next market journey.

She should have felt some guilt over snooping, but she didn't. Not at all.

This room was familiar in more than it reminded her of Finn, she realized, but because it also reminded her of her own room back home.

Nay.

A smile tugged at her lips as she stopped to stare out over the now-dark landscape.

At home, she'd shared a room with Skye her entire life, and Skye wouldn't know the meaning of "organized" if it bit her on the arse. Her clothing was hung any which way, and she was constantly searching for nick-knacks she'd put down somewhere.

But this room was organized the way Fiona *would have* organized her room, if she didn't have to worry about Skye's boots being thrown in the middle of the room, or the table being dragged around to suit whatever sparring move her twin wanted to practice at any given moment.

Staring out the open window, Fiona wrapped her arms around her middle.

Would this soon be her permanent room?

After she married Finn, would they live here together?

They obviously thought alike and were compatible…

But was that enough?

Was that enough to base a marriage on?

With a sigh, she reached for the shutter and swung it closed. Even summer nights in the Highlands could be chilly, and who knows how long it would be until Skye returned from the stables to join her in bed.

Her sister was more than a little obsessed with her horse's health, which made sense, considering how she gained money for the MacIans. But when Skye had heard what Fiona had said to Finn at supper, about leaving her door unbarred, Fiona's sister had stammered and said she'd be in the stables.

Indefinitely?

The thought of marriage might make Fiona's palms go all clammy, but the thought of *bedding* was something else entirely. Swallowing, she latched the shutter in place, wondering if Finn would come to her that evening.

Would *he* keep her warm?

She placed her hand on her neck, remembering how his lips had felt there, last year. He'd kissed her since she'd arrived at Oliphant Castle of course, but nothing like the way he'd kissed her in Wick when they'd been alone.

Like the way he might kiss her *tonight*.

She could feel her pulse pounding at the base of her throat as she dragged her hand lower. Imagining it was *him* touching her, she cupped one breast gently, trying to feel her nipple through the material of her gown.

Nay, it was too thick.

Her touch still felt good, but not as *good* as his.

In a flash, decision made, Fiona reached for the ties of her gown and wriggled out of it. As she tossed it over the chair—God help her, lust had made her as untidy as Skye!—she kicked her shoes off and reached for her breasts again.

This time, both hands cupped herself, the thin linen of her chemise all that stood between her palms and her skin.

It was...*better*. Her heart was pounding faster, *higher* somehow. Her throat was thick with wanting, as her thumbs brushed against her nipples.

Not good enough.

Dragging one hand lower, she shivered with need when her fingers swept across her stomach, then cupped her mound through her under gown.

With a moan, she dropped her head back.

And that's when the door opened.

She was standing there in the middle of the room, half-naked, cupping her tit and her cunny, and the *door opened*!

Whirling around, she wasn't sure if she was relieved, or horrified, to discover it was Finn, who was staring at her the way a starving man might eye a wheel of cheese.

Comparing yerself to cheese...?

Verra romantic.

Without a word, he stepped into the room and shut the door behind him.

Then he barred it.

Fiona's knees went weak at that blatant signal.

Then he was stalking across the room toward her, although he stopped just out of arm's reach.

Why did he stop?

Did he not want her?

Or—according to the look in his eyes—did he want her *too* much?

When he spoke, his voice was raspy. "I should've knocked. I ken that, and I apologize. I'm used to just walking in, and I cannae regret it."

She licked her lips, trying to make her voice work. "Wh— Why?"

His hungry gaze dropped to the neckline of her chemise, which had been pulled lower by her—her *touches.*

"Because then I might've missed something important."

"What's that?" she whispered.

His voice dropped to a low growl when he met her eyes once more. "The knowledge ye want me as much as I want ye."

Mayhap he would've reached for her then—Lord knew her body wanted him to, and the hunger in his eyes told her he might—had she not blurted out, "How did it go with my brother?"

When he blew out a breath and dragged one hand through his hair, she almost cursed herself.

Why had she asked that?

Because she was genuinely curious to discover if she was betrothed?

Or because she was nervous about what might soon happen between her and Finn?

Just as she opened her mouth to apologize, he turned away. He stepped toward the little shelf, his careful movements showing his control, and reached up with one finger to align the end of the ledger with the shelf's edge.

And she had to smile, as the movement was so similar to hers.

"We are no' yet betrothed," he finally said.

Fiona blurted, "Why?" before she could consider the ramifications of his words.

He sighed again as he placed his fists on his hips and tilted his head toward the ceiling. As his back faced her, she admired the taut muscles of his shoulders, but also knew it meant he was holding himself in check.

A part of her—an increasingly *big* part of her—was jumping up and down and yelling at him *not* to hold himself back.

Shut up, she told that part, *at least until I get some answers.*

"Yer brother cares for ye, Fiona."

His words were so unexpected—the fact Finn had to tell her that, not the fact Stewart cared—Fiona could only respond with something which sounded like a, "Guh?" before she could stop herself.

Now ye're making sheep sounds?

Finn hadn't turned, and she wondered if he was laughing at her.

"Stewart pointed out to my father that he—and ye—had only just arrived. He hadnae seen the two of us together long enough. He didnae ken *me* as a man, other than what ye've told him. He wants to wait to sign the betrothal contract until he's sure this is what *ye* want."

"How long will that take?"

"A few days." Finn whirled then, a haunted look in his eyes. "This *is* what ye want, is it no'?"

"Ah—" She blinked. "Aye. Of course."

"Ye hesitated."

Did she?

"Nay, I did no'."

With a nod, he started toward her, moving uncannily like a wildcat stalking its prey. The intense, *hungry* look in his eyes had

Fiona stumbling backwards, even while that part of her who *wanted* this was screaming at her to grow a backbone.

She compromised with an embarrassing little stumble before she stopped, certain that part of her was rolling its eyes.

Wait, could her subconscious roll its eyes at her?

And then she wasn't thinking at all, because he'd stopped in front of her, close enough to touch. Close enough to *smell*. Close enough she could reach up and wrap her arms around his neck and drag him down for a kiss.

If she wanted to.

I want to!

"Aye, ye did."

What in damnation were they speaking of?

"Did what?" she had to ask.

"Ye hesitated. I asked ye if this—*this*"—he gestured between them, the back of his hand brushing against her breast as he did so —"was what ye wanted, and ye hesitated."

She swallowed. "Finn," she whispered, looking into his eyes and suddenly feeling very brave—mayhap it was that part of her which was now jumping up and down in anticipation? "Finn, I can say with absolute certainty, at this moment, I want *this* verra, verra much."

The throbbing heat at her core was proof enough.

And then—thank the saints!—he placed one hand on her hip and lifted the other to brush against her neckline where the linen just barely covered her skin. She tilted her head to one side, allowing him better access.

"Are ye *sure* this is what ye want, lass?" he murmured. "No' this heat, this attraction, but a lifetime with me?"

It was hard to think when he was touching her like this. "I've only kenned ye a few days."

It wasn't an answer, but it was true.

Two days last autumn, and now she was ready to yoke herself to him for the rest of their lives?

Luckily, he had more sense than her and didn't stop touching her. "Only a few days?"

She hummed, even as she tilted her head in the other direction, as he dragged his fingertips up to the sensitive place behind her ear. He'd remembered she loved his touch there.

"Fiona MacIan, my heart has kenned yers forever."

She suspected the noise she made then, as she melted into him, was something which sounded like, "D'aww!"

And although she'd closed her eyes, she could *hear* the smile in his voice, when he said, "I've written to ye all winter. Most marriages are founded on much less."

"I ken." She swallowed and forced her eyes open. What point had she been trying to make? Oh, aye. "But do *ye* want *me*?"

His hand stilled as he reared back. "What? How could ye ask me that?"

How could I no'?

"I ken I'm no' the most beautiful woman—"

"Yer beauty has naught to do with why I love ye, lass."

With a fierce frown—for her benefit, and Fiona relished the realization that she could tell the difference—he dropped his hand to her hip, holding her in place. She didn't have time to be disappointed before he was leaning toward her.

"I love ye, Fiona MacIan. I love yer mind." Leaning close, he brushed a kiss against her forehead. "I love yer spirit." He dropped a kiss on her nose. "And I love yer heart."

This kiss he placed where it belonged—on her lips—and it was just as sweet as the one in the courtyard had been hot.

When Fiona's blood began to pound, he pulled back.

"How can ye ask if I want ye, lass?" His tone was serious as his dark eyes darted between hers. "I love ye."

"Oh, Finn," she whispered, certain she *was* melting. Her doubts were also melting right into a big puddle of desire.

And *that's* when he used his grip on her hips to pull her closer, to press her pelvis against him, allowing her to feel the great *glorious* press of his hardness against her.

Oh my.

"I want ye verra, verra much, Fiona," he said, in a choked voice.

And God help her, but she wanted him too.

Verra, verra much.

He lowered his chin so his gaze bore into hers, and she stopped breathing.

"But although I want ye *verra verra* much, I'll no' bed ye…"

Damnation!

He took a breath—a deep breath, which only served to press all of his wonderful *hardness* against her—and continued, "I'll no' compromise ye, until ye are sure ye want me in return. Want me no' just tonight, but—"

To hell with this!

With a triumphant moan, Fiona reached up, grabbed the hair over his ears, and pulled his lips down to hers.

Excellent.

Aye, this kiss *was* excellent. The way his tongue played with hers was excellent. The way his teeth grazed her lips was excellent. And his little groan of surrender was excellent too.

And then she was being lifted in the air, although she wasn't sure if that was simply another trick her mind was playing, until he dropped her onto the bed.

His bed.

His bed, where he slept each night, where *she* would sleep tonight and possibly forever, if they were married. Where he'd slept these past months, thinking of *her*.

The thought of him touching himself, the way she'd been doing when he'd walked in, had Fiona reaching for Finn to pull him down atop her.

She wore only her thin chemise, and as he covered her, she imagined she could feel *all* of him: from his hard chest to his firm stomach to his belt and his boots—

He was still wearing his boots?

When she was ready to give herself to him?

She reared up to tell him to remove his clothing, when his large hand closed around one of her breasts, and she forgot her own name.

Fiona—*My name is Fiona, right?*—arched into his touch, no breath left to even moan. *By the Virgin*, that felt delicious! And when he lowered his mouth to pull her nipple between his teeth, the sensation of the damp linen against her skin caused her vision to go black.

No, wait, that was more likely due to the lack of air.

She sucked in a lungful, her cry of, *"Finn!"* sounding desperate, even to her own ears.

He hummed against her breast, and the sensation had her squirming as she tightened her hold on his hair and pulled him closer.

With her heels planted against the bed, she pushed herself up into his hold, into his *mouth*, and wondered if she could find release without touching herself.

Oh!

Turned out, she didn't have to worry about that, because while his tongue played merry hell with her breast—*Oh good, he switched sides; the other one was getting lonely*—his free hand was suddenly on her thigh.

And, *my*, didn't those calluses feel nice, as he inched her gown upward?

His fingertips skimmed along her knee, then the inside of her thigh, until—

Until he stopped.

He froze, his mouth still attached around one nipple, and his fingers *inches* from where she wanted them.

Why in damnation did he stop?

As her hips gyrated under him, trying to press herself into his hand, Fiona lifted her head off the mattress to glare at him.

"Finn!" she finally snapped.

When he released her breast and blew out a breath, the air pressed the damp linen against her sensitive nipple and caused her to shiver in delight. He lifted his head, and she saw his eyes were screwed shut, his jaw tight.

He was moments away from losing control, and the thought made her smile.

Made her feel *powerful*.

He'd said he wasn't going to bed her—*compromise her*—until they were betrothed, but Fiona would be damned if she was letting him leave her in this state.

Making a little soothing noise—or maybe it was a yearning, desperate noise? It was hard to tell—she untangled one hand from his hair and dropped it atop his, where it rested near her thigh.

The movement caused his eyes to snap open, and she held his gaze without speaking.

Slowly, her fingers covered his, molding around them…then pulled them toward her. Toward her wetness, toward her *need*.

His eyes widened when he realized what she was doing, but she was stretched too thin to be embarrassed. She'd wanted this since last autumn, and a winter of playing with herself had only heightened her need.

Together, they pushed her chemise out of the way. Together, they cupped her aching core.

But he was the one who dragged his finger through her wetness. *He* was the one who found the bud of her pleasure nestled in the bed of curls. He was the one who pressed the heel of his hand against it, while she moaned and dropped her own hand away.

Finn was watching her, and she held his gaze, wondering what he saw on her face.

Was he holding his breath too?

And then he slid one finger inside her, and she gasped and arched against him, her need suddenly too intense to stifle.

With a groan, he dropped his head into the crook of her neck and worked his fingers against her. When he began kissing her there, she clenched the coverlet with her free hand and lifted her arse off the bed in desperation.

The pressure was building under his hand, the sensation familiar, yet at the same time, wonderfully, *wonderfully* new. She was climbing, building, ready to soar—

When a second finger slid into her, she *knew* she'd sprouted wings. With a swiftness which startled her, she jerked against him, felt her inner muscles tighten *hard* once, screamed his name, then lost herself in the intensity of her release.

It was a long moment—or possibly not, who knew?—before she opened her eyes.

When had she shut them?

When the lightening had started, mayhap?

As the world around her came into focus, she realized two things: One, she was breathing heavily, as if she'd just raced up the tower stairs to her old room. And two, Finn was staring at her.

He was lying beside her, one arm supporting himself, still fully dressed, with his *fingers inside her*. And he was staring at her as if she were the most wondrous, miraculous thing he'd ever seen.

Oh.

Finally, he blinked, then leaned forward to brush a kiss against the corner of her lips. She turned her head into the kiss, hoping for more, but he slid his fingers from her core and pulled her chemise down over her thighs.

Why did she feel lost?

How could she feel so perfectly boneless, and satiated, and *still want more*, all at the same time?

As she pondered this impossibility, he rolled onto his back and pulled her with him, nestling her in the crook of his arm, so her cheek was pillowed against his shoulder.

She felt cherished.

But from this angle, she could see, from the tenting of his kilt, *he* was very much unsatisfied.

Why?

Why had he brought *her* so much pleasure, but denied himself?

"Thank ye," he whispered.

Her head reared up. "Thank *me*? Nay, ye were the one—"

He squeezed her. "Hush, lass." With a smile, he lifted his head and kissed her temple. "That was wonderful for me, and I'll no' let ye soften it."

Soften it?

Was that a hint?

Fiona bit her lip, wondering if he expected her to return the favor. Cautiously, her hand rose, intent on reaching for his stiff member—

But he caught it and brought it to his lips. "I love ye, Fiona MacIan, and one day soon, I hope ye'll admit ye love me too."

"I do love ye, Finn," she whispered.

How could she *not*, especially after what he'd just done for her?

But why hadn't he made her his in every way?

"I hear a *but*."

She bit her lip. "Nay," she muttered.

"Aye. Ye love me, *but…*"

There was likely a time when a ghostly drummer could be annoying. Especially after the castle was dark and most were asleep. There would likely be a moment when Fiona would curse the ghostly drummer and wish the specter would pipe down.

But not tonight.

When the steady beats began to penetrate the stone walls, seeping into their chamber, she took it as a boon.

She wouldn't have to explain her feelings—complicated as they were—to Finn.

But as she sat up and met his eyes, her own wide with surprise and excitement, she was thinking of Aunt Agatha's warning:

Dooooooom!

CHAPTER 5

FINN BARELY CONTAINED his groan when the ghostly beat drifted into the room. *Just* when he thought he might be close to getting an honest answer from Fiona, *this* had to happen!

And the way she bolted upright in bed, her cheeks flushed from something besides his loving, told him she was happy for the distraction.

" *'Tis him,*" she whispered.

His forearm thrown across his eyes, Finn muttered, "I ken," as he tried to get his erection under control.

The sight of her—the *feel* of her—coming apart in his arms had been so damnably intoxicating, he'd almost spilled against her thigh. Which would've been messy. And embarrassing.

Now, just the sensation of the wool of his kilt moving against his stiff member as she shifted around in bed was enough to make him groan in frustration.

"Come along, Finn," she said, almost breathlessly.

He peeked out at her from under his arm. "Where are we going?"

He knew he sounded surly and tried to swallow down his disappointment.

It was not because he was desperate for release, nay.

It was the fact she could not admit her love for him, or lack thereof, which had him so frustrated.

But she was already out of bed, reaching for the MacIan plaid. "To find the ghost. How do I look?"

When she turned to him, Finn forced himself to sit upright in bed. Her brown hair had fallen down around her shoulders sometime since he'd entered the room to find her *touching herself*. Between that and the glow of her cheeks—not to mention the fact she stood there with her stocking toes curling into the rushes—she *looked* like a woman who had been well and truly pleasured.

Ye look like my *woman.*

But that wasn't what she was asking. With the plaid wrapped around her shoulders like that, and her chemise barely visible, she was asking if she was presentable. So he sighed.

"Ye look like a lass who was woken in the middle of the night, and set out to find the source of the drumming."

Her face split into a grin. "Excellent. And *ye* look like a helpful local lad who just happened to be passing by and decided to join in my search."

As Finn blinked down at himself—*helpful local lad?*—she dropped to her knees beside the bed.

"Lass?" Crawling to the edge, he peered down at her. "Fiona, what are ye doing?"

"Checking for the drummer," came the muffled reply.

"*Under my bed?*"

She backed out, then sat on her heels as she smiled up at him. "'Unlikely, I ken it. But 'tis better to eliminate the closest options first, before searching farther afield."

It was ridiculous to think a ghostly drummer could be in this room. On the other hand, King Edward and all his English troops might've marched through while she was in his arms, and Finn wouldn't have noticed. All he'd been able to focus on had been her face, full of joy and wonder, as he'd given her pleasure.

He had to admit he liked the methodical way she thought,

however. So he scrubbed a hand over his face, sighed, and pushed himself to the edge of the bed. "Shall I check the garderobe?"

"Yes please, and I'll check the hearth."

He was smiling when he stepped into the closet set along the outer wall, but peering down into the depth, he wasn't sure what he was looking for.

Why would a ghost be in a shite hole?

"Halloo?" Fiona called from the main room, her voice echoing up the chimney. "Anyone in there?"

She really was a delight, wasn't she?

And aye, there were things he'd *rather* be doing with her other than combing the keep for a mysterious drummer—something he and his brothers had done for years—but any time he got to spend with her wouldn't be wasted.

She was the woman he loved, and *being* with her was all that mattered.

"Come along," he said as he joined her. "Let's go check the battlements."

Which is how he found himself holding hands with the most delightful woman he knew, sneaking through the halls of his home, trying not to laugh.

"He's getting better," he murmured, reaching the door to the upper levels.

"Who?" Fiona was frowning, her ear cocked to catch the distant beats.

He pushed open the door, and tugged her outside into the cold night. "The drummer." Out here, he could speak louder, knowing the only ones to hear them would be the guards below. "When I was a lad, he couldnae hold a beat for shite. But now his rhythm is much improved."

She'd been peering over the battlement, the white linen of her chemise and her pale hair making her look a bit like a ghost herself, but now she hurried back to him. "Ye've heard him for *that* long? Yer aunt said only the doomed hear him."

"Nay, lass," he corrected, pulling her into his arms and resting his chin atop her head, "only the *doooooooomed*."

She pinched him, and he smiled.

"I mean it. Ye've heard him since ye were a lad? I dinnae believe in ghosts, of course, but…but I'm curious. I suppose I *want* to believe in ghosts. But they're no' real, aye? And I suppose I *especially* dinnae want to believe in ghosts who portend *dooooooooom*."

"As far as I'm concerned, hearing him dinnae *dooooooom* me at all." He squeezed her to let her know exactly what he meant, and he liked the way she sighed contentedly.

It was nice, up here in the chilly Highland night, his arms wrapped around the woman he loved. But as she pulled her arms from around his waist to tuck them against his chest, he felt her shiver, and knew they wouldn't find the ghost here.

"Come, lass, we'll check the undercroft," he suggested. As he pulled her back inside, he answered her question. "And aye, I've heard the drummer afore. Since we were lads, some of us could hear him, some no', depending where we were sleeping." He led her down the stairs. "The drummer only drums at night, ye ken, and has gotten more respectful of our sleep as we've gotten aulder."

Her hand gripped tightly in his, Fiona giggled. " 'Tis a polite ghost then?"

The drummer of Oliphant Castle was likely no ghost, but he was enjoying their midnight hunt too much to ruin the fun.

In the great hall, Fiona pulled him to a stop and ducked down to check under the tables.

Humoring her, he did the same on the opposite side.

"Any drummer?" she called out in a whisper.

"Naught but the hounds, irritated at being disturbed," he replied as he crossed back to her, careful not to wake any of the drunken men sleeping on the benches.

Was that Kiergan?

She took his hand when he reached her and tugged him toward the door to the undercroft. When they entered the kitchen, the banked fire gave off enough of a glow he could see her smile.

Unable to resist her allure, Finn pulled her into his arms. "Ye're enjoying yerself?"

This time, she wrapped her arms around his middle and tilted her head back to bestow her smile fully on him.

Had it only been an hour ago she'd come apart in his arms, and he'd been unable to focus on anything but his own painful arousal and her pleasure?

Well, now, his cock was polite enough not to make an appearance as he focused on the warmth her smile—her joy—caused to bloom in his chest.

"This is fun," she finally admitted. "I am tired after the day's journey, but spending time with ye like this has been a wonderful reminder of why I—"

When her eyes went wide, and she bit off the rest of her words, Finn knew what she'd been about to say. "Why ye fell in love with me?" he prompted gently.

And when she didn't answer—when she just ducked her head and pressed her lips tight—he refused to let worry or doubt claw their way into his heart.

With a sigh, he pulled her closer, tucking her head under his chin once more. There they stood, in the silent kitchen—the cook snoring softly on his pallet behind the chimney—and he felt her heart beat against his.

"Fiona, will ye tell me what ye're thinking?"

Mayhap it would be easier if they were not looking at one another.

"We only have a few memories. Together, I mean. A few days last autumn, and now…"

"Does that matter?" he asked quietly.

"Shared memories? Aye, I think 'tis an important basis for a marriage."

His nostrils flared as he considered her words. "A few moments after meeting ye, I kenned ye were the lass I wanted to marry. Remember that?"

She didn't respond, and he squeezed her gently.

"Remember the time we spent the night traipsing around my father's castle, looking for an interrupting ghost?"

Instead of laughter, he felt her sigh.

"I'm no' the most confident of women, Finn," she finally admitted. "I ken that. But still…why would someone as smart and charming and handsome as ye, want to spend yer life with someone like me?"

The answer was immediate. "I've told ye my reasons, aye? Ye're intelligent and fun, and when ye smile, I feel as if the sun has come out on a dark day. And *I* think ye're beautiful, my love."

"Ye have nae idea how helpful the reminder is…"

Again, he heard the unspoken *but*. "But?"

She sighed again. "But the doubt is eating at me."

Suddenly, he knew what they had to do.

Pulling away, he clasped her cheeks in his palms and brought his lips down upon hers.

While he hadn't intended the kiss to stir their passions, once started, it was hard to stop. She pushed herself up on her toes to draw him into the kiss, and *St. Ninian's beard*, but she felt good!

It was the sexy little whimper she gave which finally dragged him—kicking and screaming—back to his senses, and he released her lips.

They were both breathing hard when he held her gaze, wanting her to understand the seriousness of his intent.

"That's the last kiss I'll give ye, lass, until ye *stop* doubting."

"Wha—what?"

Nodding, he willed her to understand. "What I did with ye tonight—what I want to do again, even now—cannae be repeated, until ye're *sure* 'tis what ye want."

Her response was immediate. "I want it."

When she pushed her pelvis against him, he felt her heat through the thin linen, and his cock jumped in response. But he swallowed down his desire, forcing himself to be strong.

"I want it too," he admitted in a strangled whisper. "But…" Shaking his head, he tried to explain. "But ye have to want me for more than just tonight. Ye have to want me *forever*, Fiona, and ye have to trust that I want ye *forever*, as well."

She did that thing where she chewed on her bottom lip. He'd only seen her do it a few times last autumn—in the marketplace, she so rarely showed uncertainty—but it had driven him wild.

As it did now.

But it meant she was thinking, considering.

Finally, she peeked up at him, her face still cradled between his palms. "I *do* trust ye, Finn. And I love ye."

He wasn't going to make her say the *but*. Instead, he leaned down and brushed a kiss atop her nose, before releasing her completely and stepping away.

A kiss on the nose doesnae count as breaking my vow.

Right?

"Yer brother isnae willing to sign the betrothal contract until he's certain I am who ye want," he told her, hooking his thumbs in his belt to keep from reaching for her. "He's being considerate."

She looked almost forlorn as she shrugged and wrapped her arms across her belly, pulling the MacIan plaid taut across her shoulders. If he had his way, she'd be wearing the Oliphant colors for the rest of her life.

But the decision was in her hands.

"Stewart has made advantageous marriages for our older sisters," she confessed quietly. "I didnae expect him to dally in getting Skye and me married off, especially no' with his wife so close to her time. She doesnae like us much."

He was ashamed to admit he could see how someone might not like the mulish and scowling Skye, but he'd only interacted with her for any real amount of time at dinner, and she'd been glaring at him more often than not.

But Fiona?

How could anyone possibly *not* like *Fiona*?

In lack of anything to say on the subject, Finn merely shrugged. "The fact he's concerned for ye shows his affection. He told Da and me tonight he'll stay another four days, afore he must return to his wife."

From under her lowered lashes, blue flashed his way, and he took that as a good sign.

"That means ye—*we*—have four days, love. Four days to decide if this is really what ye want."

"Four days…" she repeated in a whisper.

"Aye. And Fiona?"

When she looked up at him, he captured her gaze and poured every ounce of certainty into his tone when he gave her another vow.

"I'll be using every hour of those four days to convince ye of what I already ken: We belong together."

———

TRUE TO HIS WORD, Finn was waiting for her when she came down to the great hall the next morning to break her fast. She'd slept late, because of their midnight adventures, but he didn't seem to mind.

When he saw her, he bounced to his feet with a grin and held out his hand to her. "Ye look lovely, as always."

"Thank ye," she murmured flushing. 'Twas true she'd taken care with her gown and hair that morning, enduring Skye's teasing. But seeing him in the daylight, after what they'd shared last night…

From the glint in his eyes when he smiled at her, she wondered if *he* were thinking of it too.

But instead of mentioning it, he held up a bundle. "I packed us some food, if ye'd like to go for a picnic with me?"

A picnic? What a charming idea. "*Ye* packed it?"

"Aye," he drawled with a wink, as he offered his arm for her to hold. "Ye doubt I ken my way around the kitchens?"

Heading for the main doors, she cocked her head as she considered. "Actually, I can easily imagine ye as a lad, sneaking down to the kitchens to pilfer food."

"A *lad*?" he chuckled. "I have five brothers—and Nessa's appetite is no' to be forgotten, either!—so I have to pilfer food at least once a fortnight!"

She was laughing as well as they crossed the courtyard. "Yer da tries to starve ye all, then?"

"Ach, nay. And since I'm the one who trades for our food, I dinnae want to be insulting myself. But have ye *seen* the way Rocque eats?"

"Will ye tell me about them?"

So as they meandered across a field toward a stream he claimed was a favorite, he did.

He told her how Alistair and Kiergan had lived at Oliphant Castle since they were bairns, their mother having died giving them birth. "She'd been a serving wench, as I've heard tell, so she lived in the castle anyhow. Da found a wet nurse for them, and Moira cared for them most after the nurse left."

"She's the housekeeper?"

They arrived at the spot, and he helped her to the soft, grass-covered ground.

"Aye, although she's more than that. She's cared for all of us at one point or another." He handed her a hunk of cheese, then stretched out his long legs in the cool grass beside the water. "Her son, Brohn, is like another one of us. And Lara has been Nessa's best friend since they were wee girls."

Fiona tucked her feet up under her dress and nibbled at the cheese, her attention on his lips as he spoke. She was fascinated by his family, aye, but was having a hard time thinking, when all she could remember was the feel of those lips nibbling *her*.

"Rocque and Malcolm are different. Their mother had been young, and when her father discovered she'd gotten herself with child—he told Da he'd made a whore out of her—and the bastard sent her away."

She winced at the man's cruelty, but Finn saw it and hurried to apologize.

" 'Tis no' kind to speak that way of—"

"Nay, it sounds as if he deserves worse terms."

Finn's smile flashed. "Aye, and speaking as a bastard, I'd prefer to find something else to call him."

"A devil, mayhap?"

"How about a pig?"

She tsked, enjoying their banter. " 'Tis rude to pigs."

His chuckle made her heart light.

"Well, the *muck-licking, spittle-brained swine*—how is that?—sent her away to a distant cousin, and from what Malcolm remembers, she raised them as best she could, in poor conditions. Rocque doesnae speak of that time often, and even less of what happened after she died. They came to us already half-grown, but they're our brothers, all the same."

She and Skye had a bond like that, but they were twins. What would it be like to be so close with her other siblings? To be so close in *age*, to have all been raised together?

Her own twin might look just like her, but she was a very different person. Not just in temperament and personality, or how disorganized she was either. This morning, despite her teasing, Skye had been withdrawn and distant. Fiona had the impression her sister had wanted to tell her something, but when she'd asked, Skye had just shaken her head and continued to appear worried.

But it had been hard to focus on her sister's potential upset, when she had a day with Finn to look forward to.

A day to decide if ye love him.

But 'twas foolish. She *knew* she loved him. She *knew* she trusted him.

She just had to trust him enough to believe he knew his own mind and his own heart, and that *he* loved *her*.

To distract herself from the conundrum, she reached for a slice of thick brown bread and raised her brows. "And ye and yer twin? Duncan, aye?"

"Our mother was raised in the village, an Oliphant through and through. She was young when Da met her and, well, our father's nae saint, ye understand. Apparently he had more'n a few lasses seeing to his needs that year."

"Apparently," she said drily.

"Aye, well, he made sure she had everything she needed, and we werenae a burden. When we were wee rascals, Da started spending more time with us—Alistair and Kiergan had a nurse in the castle then, remember—and eventually we moved up to the keep. Mam married the village smith, a good man, and we had a fine childhood, roaming back and forth between the two homes."

Hunger satisfied, Fiona had begun to tear the bread into pieces, which she rolled up and tossed into the stream. Watching the current pull one away, she hummed thoughtfully. "Yer Da sounds like an honorable man."

"He'd been in love, ye ken, but she died afore he could marry her. I've never asked, but got the impression he'd searched out all these lasses as a way to relieve himself during his grief."

She blushed slightly, understanding what kind of *relief* Finn meant. "And yer mother is happy?"

"Aye!" he sat up. "She gave her husband two wee lassies and a brother for me and Dunc. The lad's twelve, but he's looking to be as braw as his father."

Having met William Oliphant, and his six sons, it was hard to imagine there was anyone more *braw*, but... "I'd love to meet them."

"Ach, aye!" Slapping his forehead, Finn pushed himself to his feet and offered her his hand. "I told ye I'd take ye to meet them today. I'd also like to show ye our market, if ye'd like."

Putting her hand in his, Fiona shivered from the burst of warmth which coursed through her at his touch. "I'd like that verra much." Smiling shyly, she allowed him to pull her to her feet.

When he did, he held her a moment longer than necessary. The smoldering look in his eyes told her he wasn't regretting touching her this way, and had no intention of stopping.

But he did.

Releasing her, he stepped back, his lips tugged in a sort of rueful grimace.

"Finn?"

"I told ye I'd no' be kissing ye until ye were sure ye wanted to marry me."

Damnation.

He had, hadn't he?

Her chin came up, trying to mask her uncertainty. "And if I told ye I was ready?"

But he knew her better than that, apparently, for all that they lacked enough shared memories to build a foundation for their marriage. Shaking his head a little sadly, he tsked.

"I'd no' believe ye. No' yet. But…"

Trying to disguise her eagerness, she curled her fingers around the wool of her gown. "Aye?"

The twinkle in his eyes told her she'd failed; he'd heard how her heart had jumped at the thought of kissing him.

"*But…*" He scooped up the remainder of their picnic, and when he offered her his arm, she took it. "But do ye remember the first time I took ye to our village to show ye around? When ye stopped to admire that pretty hairpin, I bought it for ye. Ye charmed all the merchants with yer wit and smiles, and when I took ye to meet my mother's family, they loved ye as much as I."

As they began walking along the stream, heading for the distant village, Fiona felt herself smiling. She tilted her head so her temple pressed against his strong shoulder, and inhaled his scent.

He was *creating* memories for her. Memories of things which hadn't even happened yet.

And her heart swelled at the realization.

"Aye, Finn, I do recall that."

'Twould be a good way to start a marriage, a day like the one he described.

So why did she still hesitate?

CHAPTER 6

"Da, what in damnation are ye doing out here alone?"

William Oliphant straightened with a grunt and dropped the stone he'd been holding onto the pile of loosely stacked boulders, which represented a boundary wall. The older man wiped his hands on his kilt and glared up at Finn, who was still seated on his horse.

"What in damnation do ye mean, what in damnation am I doing out here? What in damnation does it *look* like I'm doing?"

With a wince, Finn worked his way through that sentence. "It *looks* like ye're trying to kill yerself." His father had passed fifty years of age, but was not an old man yet. Still, his sons liked to tease him. "If yer heart gave out when ye were out here all alone, who would think to look for ye?"

Da planted his hands on the small of his back and bent backward as he let out a breath. Finn winced again at the popping sound his father's back made and swung out of the saddle.

"First of all, laddie…" Da plopped himself down on one of the larger stones, pointing sternly at Finn's nose. "What makes ye think nae one kens I'm out here? I told Moira *and* the guards where I was heading off to. Ye ken I think physical labor sets yer mind straight when ye have a twisty problem to think through."

Humming, Finn bent down to pick up one of the stones which

had fallen from the wall. "And what kind of twisty problem do ye have, Da?"

He set the stone atop the one his father had placed, then reached for another.

"Never ye mind that, laddie. A man's problems are his own, at times. Especially when they involve women."

Women?

Finn hid the way his brows shot up by turning away and reaching for another stone. "And second?"

"What?"

This conversation was beginning to sound familiar. "Ye said *first of all*"—with a grunt, he dropped this stone beside the first—"which implies ye have at least a second point to make."

Snorting, Da shook his head. "*Second of all*, if I died out here—and I have nae intention of dying soon, but it *will* happen one day—one of ye lads would just have to step up and lead the clan."

One of us lads?

Finn wiped his hands on his kilt and sat beside his father, his eye on his horse, which had moved near Da's to investigate the sweet grass.

"That's the thing, is it no'? Da, ye're sending us off to get *married* all willy-nilly. Just because ye want a grandson."

"I want *bairns*, Finn," William corrected. "Ye ken I had a twin?"

That was news to Finn. Jerking his head around, he lowered his brows at his father. "Ye did?"

"Aye," the older man nodded. "He died shortly after we were born, so I never kenned him. But twins run in the Oliphant line, in case ye have no' noticed."

Finn snorted slightly. "Ye sired three sets of twins in less than a year, and I happen to be one of them. I *noticed*."

"Aye, well, the lassie ye've chosen as yer wife is a twin too. Which means they run in *her* family as well. Which means the two of ye are almost guaranteed to give me a set of twins by next summer!"

Groaning, Finn propped his elbows on his knees and dropped his head into his hands. "Da," he said, the words muffled, "*please* dinnae tell me ye came up with this ridiculous plan just to get grand*bairns* as fast as possible."

The mighty whack William Oliphant planted on his son's back was enough to force Finn to brace himself. And it reminded him his father was no weak old man.

"Of *course* 'tis why I came up with the plan, laddie!" his father bellowed. "I'm no' getting younger. I need some bairns to bounce on my knees and tug on my white beard!"

Finn peeked from between his fingers. "Yer beard is still as red as ever, Da. Do no' think ye can get all doddering and auld and pitiful just because ye have grandbairns."

With a wink, his father nudged him in the side. "So ye *are* getting me some grandbairns, aye? Dinnae think I missed the way ye disappeared to Lady Fiona's room the other evening."

Slowly, Finn sat up, but his gaze remained on his hands.

Aye, the evening after the MacIan party had arrived, he'd gone to his own room to meet with Fiona. And aye, he'd brought her pleasure, while simultaneously giving himself the biggest set of aching bollocks he'd ever experienced, all because he was too damn noble to take what she'd offered.

But now…?

It'd been two days since his resolve to keep his distance in that particular department. Two days he'd spent with her, every hour he could, although the evenings had ended with a chaste kiss on the back of her hand as she'd left the great hall. And he'd gone back to the barracks to flop down on his pallet and try to forget the look of longing she'd throw over her shoulder.

Two days closer to Laird MacIan's deadline, and Finn *still* didn't have an answer from her.

Could she be happy being married to him?

"Da, how come ye never remarried?"

When his father didn't answer, Finn turned his head, but didn't straighten. From this position—with his elbows still planted on his knees—Da's frown looked almost comical.

"What does that have to do with aught, laddie?"

"I think 'tis possible it has to do with *everything*, Da. We all ken ye were almost married afore—well, afore *us*. And then ye married Nessa's mother…"

With a grunt, William Oliphant pushed himself to his feet and stepped away from the wall. With his fists planted on his hips, he stared into the distance. Finn slowly straightened, eying his father's broad back.

"I married Glynnis to give ye lads a mother," Da finally admitted. "Kiergan and Alistair were living at the keep then, and ye and Duncan were in the village. I kenned I wanted ye with me as soon as yer mother was comfortable. But I also kenned ye'd need a woman's touch, a motherly sort of influence."

This was news to Finn, and he suspected his brothers as well. "So ye married…for *us*?"

"Ach, well…" Da turned and reached for another stone, smaller than the others. " 'Twas time I married anyhow. I'd been laird since I was a young man, and Aunt Agatha had been harping on me to find a bride and make an alliance." Apparently unsatisfied with the placement of the stone he'd just put atop the wall, he frowned as he made adjustments. "Of course, I'd heard the drummer a few times by then, so I thought it time."

What in damnation did *that* have to do with anything?

Finn shook his head as he focused on his father's earlier words. "Ye got another bairn out of the marriage though."

"Aye, and my Nessa is a firebrand aright."

Finn's lips twitched upward.

A firebrand?

Nessa had been raised with six brothers, only slightly older than herself. She had no notion of what it meant to be demure or quiet.

"Did ye see her latest piece?"

"Commemorating the Bruce's victory at Bannockburn? Aye, she showed me the sketches, and I believe ye'll be sending me to Inverness soon to trade for more crimson kermes dye."

Chuckling, William reached for another stone. "Aye, there *is* rather a lot of blood."

"Rather," Finn agreed drily.

His sister was an artist, with her preferred median being linen and threads. Other ladies might embroider, because society dictated they be gentlewomen, and 'tis likely why Glynnis Oliphant had insisted the lassie learn. But Nessa had taken the skill and made it uniquely her own.

That thought led to another, which led to another memory of Da's wife, and eventually Finn murmured, "Life has been more peaceful since Glynnis's passing."

Grunting in agreement, Da straightened. "Aye, why do ye think I'm in nae hurry to marry again, laddie? She was a difficult woman, who brought nae joy to those around her, including ye lads."

"But…" Finn shook his head, still trying to understand. "Ye're telling us we have to get married, though ye've never thought to remarry yerself. Ye're no' too auld to have another son."

"Mayhap." The older man turned away, studying the length of the stone wall, what remained of it. "But I *am* too auld to be *raising* another son. I've raised ye lads well enough, and I expect one of ye to take over after me. Just as I expect the rest of ye to support yer laird."

Finn stared down at his hands. He and his brothers hadn't been raised to think they'd be the next Oliphant Laird. Is that why reactions to Da's command had been so mixed?

"What are ye thinking, Finn?" his father asked quietly, still not looking at him. "Ye and yer brothers, do ye no' want to marry? To become laird?"

Finn answered truthfully. "Reactions are mixed. Kiergan is against it, but an idiot could've told ye that'd be his response. Rocque would make a strong laird, Malcolm a smart one—if he could leave his inventions long enough. Alistair is the one who's been running this clan for the last few years already."

"What about Duncan?"

Sighing, Finn shrugged. "Dunc has only ever wanted one thing. If I had to guess, I would say the reason he's still no' back from Larg yet is because he's avoiding ye and avoiding the issue. If he can put off marrying long enough, one of the rest of us will present ye with a grandson first, and he'll be free to do what he wants."

He and Duncan might be identical, but they were different enough, the clan had long ago learned to tell them apart by personality alone. That, and the fact Dunc was often scowling.

Da's strong arms crossed in front of his chest as he turned back to Finn. "I've told him he'll marry this year, and he *will*." When Finn merely shrugged, Da's scowl eased. "And *ye*, laddie? Ye're the first of all of ye to marry. Are ye looking forward to being the next Laird Oliphant?"

"Honestly?" Finn shook his head as he stood up and shook out his hands, suddenly full of uncomfortable energy. "I dinnae ken." He began to pace, thinking aloud. "I've never wanted to be laird, and ye've given me everything I could want when ye promised me a place as the clan's trader."

Reaching the horses, he patted his on the shoulder, thinking of the possibilities.

And what needed to happen first.

"Ye said Rocque would be a strong laird, but there's benefits to a *charming* one too, Finn," the older man said quietly. "Ye'd make a fine laird, merely because ye never expected the power."

"I'd have to be married first," Finn murmured.

"Ah." There was silence from behind him for a moment, then Da said, "So *that's* what sent ye out here today? No' just looking for an auld man to give him grief about working alone to clear his head?"

Leave it to Da to make a joke out of this. With a snort, Finn began pacing again, the words falling out of his mouth before he could stop them.

"I fell in love with Fiona the day I met her; I kenned I wanted her as my wife. And though she says she loves me, she hasnae given her heart to me. And with her brother giving her the choice, I havenae earned her promise she'll marry me."

Humming, his father dropped his thumbs to his belt. "And ye're sure she loves ye?"

"*Yes.*" Finn stopped short and dragged his hands through his hair.

"Nae. Ach, I dinnae ken, and 'tis what's driving me mad. She *says* she does, and she has all winter. So why will she no' commit to a lifetime with me?"

He knew he was whining. He *knew* he'd come out here for his father's advice. And now that he'd vomited all his woes at Da's feet, Finn held his breath and prayed the older man would have answers.

He didn't.

"Marriage is no' everything, laddie. Glynnis taught me that," William said, almost sadly. "If she's no' the one, then I dinnae want to push ye into—"

"Fiona MacIan is the one for me, Da. I'll marry her tomorrow if she'll have me."

Da hummed. "Ye need passion."

"We *have* passion." What they'd shared that first night, in his own chambers, proved that. The way her glances made his blood pound and his cock throb proved it too. "Passion isnae our problem."

"Ye need respect, son. Ye have to care for one another, and care *about* one another. Ye're certain ye can see yerself caring for this lass for the rest of yer life?"

His mouth opened to declare *"Aye!"* but something stopped Finn. He crossed his arms in front of his chest, and stared over his father's shoulder as he considered the older man's question.

Fiona was a good woman, a *kind* woman. Everything he knew of her told Finn that. Even if they didn't love one another, kindness and caring would be a good way to start a marriage. A solid foundation.

And he respected her, enough to allow her the decision about their marriage, even though he would've said *aye* and signed the contract days ago.

But did *she* respect *him*?

She cared for his opinion and deferred to him when they were with others. She'd *treated* him with respect. But more importantly, she'd treated *everyone* around her with respect.

So aye, she was respectful and kind and caring. A solid foundation for a marriage.

Finn frowned, thinking of his father's marriage. He'd married Glynnis when Finn and his brothers were wee lads, and she'd ruled the Oliphant keep for years before dying in an attempt to bring another bairn into the world. *She* had treated no one with respect, and although she might've once been sweet and beautiful, bitterness and anger had turned her unkind and harsh.

That was Da's experience with marriage.

That was why he'd avoided marrying again, Finn was sure of it.

And 'twas why he now asked these questions.

So Finn lifted his chin and met his father's eyes again. "Aye, Da." Fiona was nothing like his stepmother. "Aye, I would be happy married to her for the rest of our lives. She's a good woman."

"Och, well, then…"

William Oliphant shrugged as he closed the distance between them to pound on Finn's shoulder again, then drop one still-meaty arm around the younger man's shoulders.

"I cannae tell ye how to make the lovely lass marry ye, laddie. *Ye're* the charmer of the family." Da gave him a little shake, which managed to make Finn feel comforted *and* dizzy all at once. "If anyone can convince Lady Fiona she needs a lifetime with ye…'tis *ye*."

It wasn't exactly helpful, but Da's advice *was* somehow comforting.

Finn dropped his arms to pat the older man's shoulder. "Thanks, Da. No' what I wanted to hear, but thanks."

"Ach, well, if I told ye what ye wanted to hear, instead of what ye *needed* to hear, I'd be a piss-poor father."

"I'll remember that for when I'm a father."

"Write it down, son." Da winked. "I'm full of gems of wisdom like that. Like how I taught ye to piss off the curtain wall, remember?"

"That was Kiergan ye taught, but aye, I remember the way ye damn near fell over from laughing."

The older man chuckled. "I taught ye to hold a sword and how to fish. I've given ye plenty of fine advice over the years."

"Da, ye once told me fairies burrowed in cow shite, and I spent a fortnight digging through piles to catch one."

Now his chuckles turned to outright guffaws, as Finn's father released him and slapped him on the back. "See? Fine parenting there. Between that, and telling ye about the *intestinal disturbance* raw poultry is likely to cause ye—"

"That was Rocque, and he learned it the hard way."

"*I'm a fine father*, is what I was trying to say."

Then, to Finn's surprise, the older man's expression sobered as he met Finn's eyes. "I've no' told any of ye often enough, but I love all seven of my children, and I only want the best for all of ye. I'll tell ye this much, laddie…"

It was the seriousness in Da's gaze which had Finn swallowing and stepping toward him. "Aye?"

"Lady Fiona will make ye a fine wife. The saints themselves know if she'll make ye laird, but if she *does*, she'll be a fine Lady Oliphant. Ye love her, ye feel passion for her, and ye respect her. 'Tis what makes a solid marriage, I would think."

It took Finn a moment to make his voice work. Dropping his chin in acknowledgement, he whispered, "Thanks, Da."

In a blink of an eye, his father had straightened, humor back in his expression, as he bellowed, "Ye just have to wait until *she* realizes that! But dinnae keep me waiting long, laddie! I'm ready to meet yer twins! I'm thinking one lassie and one grandson!"

Finn rolled his eyes. "Thanks, Da," he repeated, sarcastically.

William Oliphant slapped the back of his hand against Finn's chest. "Now quit moping and get yer skinny arse over here to help me move the rest of these damned rocks!"

CHAPTER 7

THREE DAYS.

Three days since Finn had given *her* control over their futures.

Three days since he'd shown her he trusted her and respected her decision.

Three days since he'd *kissed* her.

Any guesses as to which was preying on her mind the most?

With a sigh, Fiona forced a smile and a polite nod for the guards at the gate, hoping they wouldn't see her frustration.

Her *longing*.

Her intense irritation that Finn had held her in his arms and made her explode in a million tiny pieces, and *then* put her back together again by being so sweet and wonderful, but now, *wouldn't do it again!*

As she made her way down the slope to the village heart, that annoying part of Fiona's mind, which wouldn't shut up, was rolling its non-existent eyes again.

Lass, ye're *the one who willnae commit to* him. *Ye're the reason he's holding himself back.*

He hadn't even *kissed* her again, damn it!

Months and months of being stuck inside by the winter snows, months of poring over each and every one of his letters until she could practically *smell* him…here she was *with him*, and he'd brought her the most incredible climax of her life, and *he wouldn't even kiss her.*

And it was her own damnable fault.

So was it any wonder she was angry at herself?

She *wanted* to commit to the man. She wanted to tell him she loved him, and he was everything she wanted in a husband, and *of course* she'd marry him.

She wanted to kiss him again.

So why hadn't she?

Three days…

When she reached the village square, she plastered on a smile and returned the polite greetings of the Oliphants. Because if she could *just make herself commit, damn it*, these people would be her people too.

The little yard behind the blacksmith's shop was empty, so she poked her head inside. Edward Oliphant, Finn's stepfather, was pounding away at his anvil with one of his large hammers. Across the shop, young Ned was making…sticks?

Finn's younger half-brother looked up from his work, and his face lit with an innocent grin. "Ye came back, milady! Would ye like to watch me make nails?"

Nails, huh? That's what those things were supposed to be?

With a smile—a genuine one this time—Fiona stepped into the shop and crossed to the twelve-year-old. This small forge was where Finn's twin brother Duncan often worked with his silver and gold…judging by the cot tucked along the back wall, he slept here as well, to protect his work.

"Aye, Ned, of course I'd like to see ye make a nail. Can ye show me how 'tis done?"

The lad was as enthusiastic as his father was taciturn. From across the shop, Edward nodded politely to her, but didn't stop his work. She waggled her fingers in a return greeting, but then gave his son her full attention when the lad launched into a narrated process.

Two days ago, Finn had brought her here to introduce her to his family. And, just as he'd promised, they'd made *memories*. She'd met his kind, though seemingly tired mother, Elsa, his two giggling sisters, and young Ned, before Edward had returned from the smithy. And it seemed as though Finn had sent word ahead, because despite their morning picnic, Elsa had had a meal prepared for them to share.

There'd been much teasing and laughter, and Fiona had been surprised to find herself just as at home in the little blacksmith's cottage, as she'd been among Finn's boisterous brothers each evening at dinner.

As she ducked out of the way of a particularly enthusiastic swing of Ned's hammer, Fiona reflected on the fact the only member of Finn's family she hadn't yet met was his brother, Duncan.

'Twas strange that the man was still away from the keep, especially with Finn's deadline approaching.

After she'd been sufficiently impressed by Ned's nails—three times, actually, because he offered her one as a keepsake—she stopped him with a teasing grin.

"And where are yer sisters this afternoon, Ned? They're no' learning the smithing trade with ye?"

"Ach, nay." The lad rolled his eyes and dropped his hammer into its sling, his exasperation making him look even more like his father. "Da says if he dinnae have a son, he'd have an apprentice, and the lassies would likely never leave the smithy, in case his apprentice took his shirt off."

Fiona lifted her hand to her lips to cover her grin, wondering if the lad even knew what he was referencing.

"Instead, they're over at the carter's, likely," Ned continued with a scowl. "Da says the *carter's* apprentices are lazy good-fer-naughts, and the lassies could do better with a blind donkey and a lame mule."

Oh heavens.

"But the carter's apprentices take their shirts off, I'll wager?"

Ned slapped his hand against his thigh and nodded enthusiastically. "One of them has arms as big around as my *head*! And he's only sixteen!"

"Hmmm. I think I can guess why yer sisters spend so much time over there." Before the lad could launch into another of his father's mimicked rants, she hurried to ask, "Is yer mother at home?" She lifted the bundle she'd brought along, wrapped up to keep clean. "I would like to visit with her."

"Ned!" the lad's father bellowed across the shop, "I need five dozen nails before supper!"

The lad waved to his father, then grinned unrepentantly at Fiona as he picked up the hammer again.

"Aye, Mam's in the house, far as I ken. She'll be happy to see ye again, milady!"

Fiona returned his smile with a little wave. "Good luck getting all the nails done, Ned."

"Nae problem! I'm already on number thirty!"

As she crossed the small yard to the door of the smith's cottage, Fiona heard the sound of two hammers striking anvils and smiled to herself. Edward the smith was not an emotive man, but 'twas clear he cared for his family's livelihood.

Did Elsa love him?

The question surprised her. Elsa was Finn's mother; what did it matter if she loved her husband?

Well, for one, knowing whether she did or no' might help Fiona understand what in damnation *she* was feeling.

When Elsa opened the door to her knock, Fiona was so lost in her thoughts, she startled and jumped.

"Hello, milady. Can I help ye?"

Shaking herself, Fiona smiled. "Nay—well, aye. I was hoping ye had a moment or two to visit. But if ye're busy, I can come back—"

But Elsa was already opening the door wide. "A nice afternoon visit—and a chance to sit down—is just what I need. Come in, milady."

"I brought ye—" Flushing, she held the bundle out to her hostess.

"When I kenned Finn's mother lived nearby, I wondered if ye might like this length of silk. As a gift."

The older woman gasped happily and pulled the yellow material from the basket, holding it up. " 'Tis beautiful, milady. Thank ye for yer kindness."

Fiona's flush deepened. "Thank *ye* for raising such a wonderful man."

Judging from Elsa's grin as the woman carefully folded her gift, 'twas the right thing to say. But then, the older woman surprised her.

"I birthed the lads, but cannae take credit for raising them myself, ye ken, milady."

"Please call me Fiona," Fee murmured, as she followed Elsa to the cottage's table.

Elsa gestured for her to sit, then bustled about, pouring two mugs of tea. "Ach, if ye're to be married to my son, I suppose I'll have to get used to calling ye by yer Christian name, aye?"

Blowing on her tea, Fiona murmured something noncommittal, hoping it would pass.

It didn't.

Elsa's too-shrewd eyes were watching her.

"Ye *are* planning on marrying my son, are ye no', Fiona?" she asked gently.

Fiona shifted in her seat.

As if understanding she couldn't answer right away, Elsa hummed and picked up her own tea in both hands. "Ye ken, we met yer sister yesterday."

Thankful for the change in subject, Fiona raised her brows. "Ye did? She was in the village?"

I've been wondering where she'd gone.

Skye had been avoiding her these last three days. At least, that's the way it felt. Her sister had been awkward whenever they *were* together, asking careful questions about her feelings for Finn, then not meeting her eyes when Fiona told the truth.

Fiona assumed her sister was keeping some sort of secret, but had been too wrapped up in her own conundrum to ask. Now she wondered if the village had something to do with it.

Elsa sipped from her tea. "No' just the village; she came to the smithy when I happened to be there. She was there to ask about *caltrops*, of all things. Wanted to ken if Edward had sold any recently to strangers."

Fiona frowned slightly, hoping the steam from the tea would hide it.

Caltrops?

She knew some of Skye's men preferred the use of the dangerous little devices, but couldn't imagine Skye agreeing to harm a horse by using them.

"Of course," Elsa said with a shrug, "we thought she was ye. The two of ye really are as alike as reflections, ye ken. Just like my lads."

"Duncan and Finn look so much alike?"

"Och, aye." Elsa waved away the question as she set her mug down. "But that should've just given us a hint earlier." Her lined face crinkled with a grin. "Poor Edward talked to her for ten minutes, thinking she was the same lass Finn had brought to dinner the day afore!" She was chuckling as she shook her head. "I was the one who finally figured it out, poor dears."

Fiona was chuckling along by that point, imagining her sister trying to bluster her way through a meeting where the smith's family would've been acting so strangely.

'Tis a pity she didnae think to tell ye of the mix-up herself.

The thought abruptly put an end to Fiona's humor, and she put the mug down with a sigh, only to realize Elsa was watching her intently.

Unable to meet the older woman's eyes, Fiona dropped hers to her half-finished tea once more.

The silence stretched, until finally, Elsa clucked her tongue and stood with a sigh. "I have to chop the onions for tonight's stew, but I dinnae mean to push ye away."

Before Fiona could do more than place her hands on the table, ready to stand and make her goodbyes, the older woman waved her back into her seat.

"Just sit yerself there, *Fiona*, and sip yer tea, while ye come up with the bollocks to tell me why ye came to visit me." She returned to the table with a knife and a handful of onions, and pierced Fiona with a sharp look. "Because I doubt 'twas my company ye were after."

"I enjoy yer company verra much."

Fiona's protest sounded weak to her own ears, and the older woman just hummed.

The knife came down a few times, slicing the vegetables with precision, and the smell began to waft through the small cottage. After a few awkward moments, Fiona was surprised to hear Elsa sniff.

Alarmed, her gaze flew to the older woman, and she saw tears threatening to spill from Elsa's eyes.

"*Elsa?*"

Sniff. "Aye?" The knife came down hard again on the onions.

"Are ye… Are ye aright?" Fiona prodded cautiously.

The older woman's chin jerked up, as her tears finally spilled. "What?"

It must've been the way Fiona was staring at her—she imagined it was a look halfway between horror and concern—which finally told Elsa what the problem was.

With a burst of laughter, the older woman dropped the knife and wiped her cheeks with her sleeve, tears still flowing.

"I'm aright, dear. 'Tis just the fate of onions…so bloody sad, ye ken."

Well, Fee hadn't expected *that* jest. Her laughter—half relieved—burst out of her, even as her own nose wrinkled from the smell of chopped onions.

While Elsa was blinking frantically, trying to recover, Fiona stood and crossed to the front door. "May I open this to let in fresh air?"

"Please," Elsa sniffed gratefully. "I always forget when chopping the damned things!"

Standing in the open doorway, Fiona inhaled deeply until she felt in less danger of crying. By the time she returned to the table, Elsa was no longer crying, and had finished chopping most of the onions.

As she slid back into her chair and reached for her tea, Fiona tried to think of a way to steer the conversation back where she wanted it. "Now I see where Finn gets his sense of humor from. His mother."

Elsa hummed. "Thank ye. But I'm no' just *Finn's* mam, ye ken. I have four other children. But Duncan and Finn were my first, and I'm grateful for how things worked out for them."

Fiona curled her hands around the mug and sat forward, anxious to know more, but also hating how useless she felt.

"Finn said ye were young when ye caught the laird's eye—I mean, when ye had them."

To her surprise, Elsa propped her hip against the table and smiled fondly into the distance, the knife still gripped in her hand.

"Ach, I was a bonny lass then. My girls look like me, thank the saints. I'd lived here in the village my whole life, and knew the Oliphant from back when he was just *William*, the laird's son." She sighed, her smile turning wistful. "The puir man ached fiercely when his lady love died. I ken I wasnae the only one he turned to for comfort, but I was game."

"And when ye discovered ye were carrying his bairns?"

"Well, I only thought 'twas *one* bairn," Elsa corrected with a laugh. "When that maid up at the castle birthed his twins, I became a little nervous. My own mam dinnae help, either, with all her horror stories of the birthing chamber!"

Fiona winced in sympathy, but couldn't help but be caught up in the woman's fonder memories. "I can imagine 'twas a surprise!"

"I recall the midwife yelling 'twas a boy, and I was so relieved to be done with it...until the pains started up again!" Elsa was chuckling. "*Two* fine lads, healthy as spit, and born within minutes of one another."

Was spit healthy then?

"Which one was aulder?"

The older woman shrugged, reaching for the onions once more, still smiling. "I dinnae think anyone kept track, and it dinnae matter to me. That first year's memories are hazy, ye ken, but the laird was there to visit his lads every chance he got."

There was something about Elsa's smile, the look in her eyes, which made Fiona wonder if the woman had always cared for William Oliphant, at least on some level. Certainly, the man visiting her bairns and offering financial support, made him sound like a good, kind man.

With her attention on her task, Elsa continued her story. "There'd been a time I might've thought we had a chance at a future, the laird and I. But he was still mourning then, and I kenned he needed a wife with grand connections. I think he did too, but he was too wrapped up in being a father to my lads and the two up at the keep."

"And once they were weaned, Finn said they spent more time with their father?"

Elsa hummed in agreement as she scooped half the onion pieces up and crossed to the pot bubbling near the fire. "By the time they were four, the whole village and castle kenned they'd roam as they pleased. There was a nurse up there who tried to keep them straight, but she'd have better luck caging falcons. Those lads were wild."

It was obvious from the fondness in her tone that Elsa didn't see that as a bad thing. "And what about ye?"

"Ach, I was wild too!" Elsa sent her a wink as she crossed to the table to gather the rest of her vegetables. "Thanks to the laird's generosity, I didnae *have* to work, and the local lads started paying me more attention. I was a prize in those days," she ended with a sigh, as she dumped the remaining onions in with the rest and picked up the spoon to give the stew a stir.

"I think ye're still a prize, Elsa," Fiona said with a quiet sigh.

The older woman sent her a soft smile. "Ye're a good lass. Have ye worked out why ye're here?"

Nay, no' yet.

"Tell me about Edward," Fiona blurted instead, not sure she was ready to ask her real questions.

"He's a good man," Elsa said softly, turning her attention to the stew. It seemed as if she wouldn't say more, but after a few moments, changed her mind. "I've kenned him since we were bairns. He's braw and brash, aye, but honorable. He respects me, and 'tis important."

Respect.

Finn had shown Fiona over these last few days—and in his letters—he respected her.

"My lads were six when Edward courted me. I wasnae sure what to make of him at first, but 'twas the way he treated Finn and Duncan that convinced me."

"What do ye mean?" Fiona pushed her mug aside and propped her chin in her hands.

Elsa crossed the room again, reaching for a rag to clean up the mess from her chopping. "He was patient with them, and I was impressed. Finn has always cared more for *people* than objects, but my Duncan has an eye for beauty Edward kenned he could bring out. Dunc's first time picking up a hammer was under Edward's watchful eye, and although the lads lived up at the keep, he always made time to teach Duncan what he wanted to learn."

"But Duncan isnae a blacksmith, is he?"

"Nay, he's a *gold*smith," Elsa said proudly. "The Oliphant would likely rather his sons grow to be strong warriors, and Duncan can handle a sword as well as the next. But his real passion is in *creating*. He shapes silver and gold into the most beautiful works ye've ever seen." Fumbling for her neckline, Elsa pulled out a chain with a lovely silver pendant in the shape of a flower, and held it up. "When he is working, or speaking of his work, ye can *see* his passion for it."

" 'Tis beautiful," Fiona murmured, although her attention wasn't on the piece of jewelry.

Instead, she sat back in her chair and pursed her lips.

Passion.

It wasn't until Elsa hummed in agreement, that Fiona realized she'd said the word aloud, and decided to just come out and *ask*.

"And how about ye and Edward? Did ye find passion together?"

Elsa stared at her a moment, before pulling out a chair and sliding into it. Facing Fiona, she took a deep breath. "Our marriage might no' be perfect, and we might no' go at it as if we were rabbits, but 'tis no' what's important."

Rearing back, Fiona studied the other woman, remembering the way Finn's hands on her body made her feel. Remembering the way just *the memory* of his hands made her feel.

"No' important?" she repeated incredulously.

And Elsa shook her head. "Passion and lust *is* important. But as the mother to two of the laird's bastards, let me tell ye, *passion* will no' last for the rest of yer lives. *Marriage* is what is important. Marriage is what will last."

Hmm.

Frowning, Fiona dropped her gaze to her hands clasped in front of her on the table.

Marriage is what is important.

Finn had offered, not just passion, but *marriage*.

And she'd hesitated.

"Fiona," the older woman said gently, "with Edward, I have a man I trust and respect; a man to share life's burdens with. I have three fine children by him, and he cares for us all."

"*Cares* for?" Fiona blurted, jerking her gaze to the older woman's. "Is it no' *love* ye should feel for yer husband?"

Elsa smiled gently. "What is love, if no' working hard to provide for yer husband or wife? What is love, if no' asking their opinion and respecting it, or defending them to others? What is love, if no' kenning each other's likes and dislikes, and going out of his way to make ye happy, and ye doing the same? What is love, if no' holding one another when ye lose a bairn, his tears mixing with yers, or worrying over yer lassies' prospects, or the gentleness in his large hands when he brushes yer hair from yer eyes?" Elsa shook her head, her smile growing. "Marriage—a commitment to one another, a *partnership*—*is* love, Fiona."

Slowly, Fiona felt herself smiling in return, not bothering to hide the tears in her eyes.

Elsa might've felt something—*love?*—for William Oliphant at one point. Certainly there'd been enough passion there between the two of them to create Finn and his brother.

But that passion hadn't lasted, despite the fact the laird was a good man. He hadn't offered her marriage. He hadn't offered her a lasting commitment or partnership.

Edward the smith *had*.

Sitting there at a humble table in a small cottage, Fiona understood what this woman was trying to tell her about building a life with another person.

Marriage will last.

Finn hadn't just offered her passion. He hadn't just offered her *his heart* and his love.

He'd offered her marriage. A commitment.

And *that* was what was important.

Elsa reached across the table and took Fiona's hand in hers. "Do ye love my son, lass?"

Eyes still wide from her realizations, Fiona shook her head. Then she contradicted herself by nodding. "I *do*. I do love him. I just wasnae certain I wanted to marry him."

"And now?"

Fiona's fingers tightened around this woman's, this woman who would be her mother-in-law one day soon, and she smiled. She smiled because she couldn't contain the joy bubbling up inside of her.

"Now...I *am* certain."

CHAPTER 8

"...WHICH would be easier if it weren't so blasted *cold* all the time."

His aunt's hand tucked in the crook of his arm, Finn hummed distractedly as they shuffled slowly across the courtyard toward the keep's steps. " 'Tis summer, Aunt Agatha."

The old woman's cane came down hard on the packed dirt, as she spat out, "Bah! 'Tis only summer because the calendar *says* 'tis summer, when clearly 'tis spring, or possibly still winter." With an exaggerated shiver, the older woman paused to adjust her arisaid.

Chafing at the slow pace, Finn still managed to nod in commiseration and help her pull the wool higher on her shoulders. "But the calendar is what tells us the seasons, Aunt. And it says 'tis summer."

"But who *makes* the calendar, laddie, hmm?" She squinted, then nodded in satisfaction. "The *men*. And after a lifetime here on earth, I can tell ye, men are idiots."

Tugging her gently into motion—*slow* motion—once more, Finn hid his smile. "Well, speaking as a man, I feel as if I ought to—"

His aunt made a dismissive noise and interrupted him, saying, "No' *ye*. Ye're still young enough I can teach ye to use yer brain."

"And claim 'tis winter, despite Beltane having come and gone?" Finn asked blandly.

"Exactly."

They were almost to the steps. "I shall endeavor to think criti-
cally, madam."

The dear old bat then *pinched* him.

"Dinnae take that charming tone with me, laddie. All of ye are
clot-heids, until a good woman gets a hold of ye. Dinnae think I
havenae noticed ye moping about since Fiona arrived, and I'm well
aware of yer little self-imposed deprivation."

At the mention of Fiona's name, Finn's head had jerked up, but
his aunt's cryptic remark had him wincing.

Was it possible she *did* understand the vow he'd made to himself
to not kiss Fiona again, until she was ready to become his wife?

The vow he'd regretted every hour for three straight days?

He'd done everything he could to show his love he was ready to
build a life with her, but this afternoon, she'd been distracted when
she'd asked for some time alone to think. The guards had seen her
heading toward the village with a bundle, and it'd been a struggle to
keep from going after her.

She wanted to be alone.

So instead, he'd offered himself as an escort for his great-aunt's
constitutional, a duty he was beginning to regret.

Now, under her disconcerting squint, he swallowed and shifted
his weight, wondering how quickly he could deposit her indoors
and escape. "I dinnae ken what ye're talking about."

Agatha scoffed. "Ye're no' a *complete* idiot, laddie, despite being a
man. Just think about it for a moment—"

"Finn!"

Politeness dictated he ignore all distractions when he was
focused on his great-aunt. She deserved his respect, and he should
be attentive to her words.

But *politeness* could go piss into a high wind, because Finn had
recognized that voice.

Aunt Agatha's arm still tucked into his, he spun around, which
caused the old lady to shuffle faster than she was used to. He didn't
care, because Fiona was running toward him, and something was
wrong.

Dropping his aunt's arm, he lunged for Fiona, and they crashed together in the center of the courtyard.

"Fiona?" His eyes searched her face as he patted her shoulders and arms, looking for the emergency. "What's amiss, lass? What is it?"

And that's when he finally realized she was smiling. Not just smiling, but *smiling*; her joy lighting up her entire face.

Her joy lit *his* heart.

"Fee?" his whispered, freezing in place.

Her hands caught his cheeks, and she pulled him down, her lips claiming his.

'Tis no' breaking a vow if she kisses me, aye?

And then he wasn't thinking, wasn't trying to rationalize anything, because her tongue swept across the seam of his lips and he closed his arms around her to pull her closer, taking command of the kiss with a deep, surrendering groan.

Who knows how long he might've stood there, kissing her under all the Oliphant eyes?

But when something slammed against the back of his knee, hard enough to cause it to buckle, he jerked away from Fiona.

Acting on instinct, he blocked her from danger with his body, and twisted...only to find his great aunt glaring up at him when he turned.

"Did ye just kick me on the back of my knee?"

"Nay," she said innocently. "I whacked ye with my cane."

"Finn?" Fiona's confused whisper came from behind him.

He shook his head, still glaring at his great-aunt. "Why would ye whack my knee with yer cane?"

She shuffled closer. "Because I could no' reach the back of yer head. And despite how athletic I clearly am, I couldnae seem to make my legs work well enough to kick ye."

Exhaling slowly, he tightened his hold on Fiona, but shifted to pull her into the conversation as he struggled to maintain his calm. "I meant, *what cause did I give ye* to hit me at all?"

"Ach, that," the old woman scoffed. She waved her hand dismissively before dropping it to the handle of the cane. "No' only were the pair of ye making fools of yerselves, sucking on each other's faces as if ye were completely out of yer own air to breathe…but 'tis obvious ye just broke whatever promise ye'd made to yerself."

Rearing back, Finn exchanged a puzzled look with Fiona, who shrugged, the earlier light in her eyes having now turned to confusion.

"What vow?" he asked cautiously, remembering his aunt's earlier words and wondering if the old woman had a way of *knowing*.

Agatha clucked her tongue. "I ken ye, laddie. When ye thought yer true love was coming here to be yer wife, ye looked as if ye might sprout wings and fly at any given moment. Happier than a hedgehog in a raspberry tart, ye were. And when she was by yer side that first night, ye were prouder than a hound who'd treed a goat."

Finn frowned, trying to make sense of her words.

Which obviously was a mistake, because she whacked him with her cane *again*!

"*Focus*, laddie! That night the drummer played, remember? And ye've been moping ever since."

"Nay…"

Pulling Fiona backwards, out of Agatha's reach, he tried to soothe his irritation, so his great-aunt wouldn't see it showing clearly on his face. Though he loved the old bat, he began to pray that one of his brothers—or *anyone*—would come along right then, so he could be alone with Fiona.

Agatha planted both hands on her cane and glared at him. "Dinnae deny it, laddie. 'Tis clear as the nose on yer face ye've been affected by the drummer. 'Tis clear ye made some sort of promise no' to kiss the lass, judging by how many hungry looks ye've sent her way without acting on them. *So* I hit ye in order to remind ye no' to break yer vows."

Damnation.

Had he really been so obvious?

Wincing, Finn tightened his hold on Fiona and lifted his leg to rub at the place his aunt had hit him. "Thank ye, I suppose. 'Twas no' entirely planned, ye ken. I'd only vowed no' to kiss Fee until she agreed—"

To become my wife.

Sucking in a frantic breath, he whirled, both hands going to Fiona's hips and dragging her away from him far enough he could duck his chin and meet her eyes clearly. "Fee?"

This time her smile was shy, but still full of excitement as she lowered her lashes over twinkling eyes.

"Fiona MacIan," he struggled to get the words past the rasp in his throat, "why did ye kiss me?"

"Because I love ye," she whispered.

"Ach, *dooooooom!*"

Both Finn and Fiona jerked, startled by his aunt's interruption, and turned to frown at her.

Agatha was smiling. "*Dooooooooooooooom!* 'Tis what the drummer foretells, aye?"

It took two tries to get his throat to work. "Ye think we're doomed, because I've heard him?"

"Aye! Doomed to fall in love! 'Tis the curse of the Oliphant Drummer! *Dooooooooooom!*"

He blinked, his gaze falling on Fiona. Her smile was back, and it was impossible to miss the excitement in her eyes.

"Lady Agatha," she began cautiously, "are ye saying the Oliphant Drummer is only heard by those destined to fall in love?"

The old woman rolled her eyes and smacked the end of her cane against the ground. "What the hell *else* would I mean? Isnae falling in love enough *doooooooooom* for ye?"

Finn groaned, dropping his head back. "For fook sake's Aunt Agatha, *seriously?*"

But Fiona was giggling.

"Aunt Agatha, ye'll be late for supper," a voice called out from the direction of the keep.

Finn could've *kissed* Kiergan when his half-brother ambled up and took their aunt's arm.

"Allow me to escort ye inside, while my clumsy brother figures out how to woo a woman."

Aright, maybe he'd not *kiss* him.

Accepting Kiergan's help, Agatha waved her cane briefly, encompassing both Finn and Fiona, the keep, and most of the courtyard. "Aye, I'm hungrier than a tortoise at market. But I couldnae go in until I explained about the Oliphant Drummer to this idiot."

Already leading the old woman toward the stairs, Kiergan threw a mocking smile over his shoulder. "Ye mean he *still* hasn't figured it out?"

Definitely no' kiss.

He was scowling after the pair when Fiona's hand landed on his cheek, and she turned his face to hers...and his mood immediately lightened.

"If we hadn't fallen in love already, the drummer sealed our fate," she whispered with a smile.

"Aye, we were *doooooomed* from the beginning, I guess."

"Ye *did* say ye heard him last year, before ye met me in Wick."

His hands went to her hips again. "Aye, I've heard him other times. Since I was a lad, really," he murmured, pulling her closer.

Fiona's hands settled on his shoulders, and her smile grew. "Then I guess we could say ye were doomed to love me from the beginning."

"Fee"—how had his lips ended up so close to hers?—"I *do* love ye."

"Then kiss me," she whispered.

Did that mean...?

"Fiona," he managed in a strangled whisper, "ye ken I promised no' to kiss ye until ye agreed to be my wife."

"Aye." Her eyes twinkled as she tugged him down. "*So kiss me,*" she whispered.

It was the joy—the *promise*—in her eyes which told him she was giving him *her* vow.

As his heart leapt with excitement, he slammed his lips down atop hers.

And her little moan of pleasure, the way she pressed herself closer, the way he felt her warmth and arousal and anticipation, told him she was *his*.

Now, and forever.

CHAPTER 9

"Do ye no' need to check on yer horse?"

Fiona held her sister's shawl out to her and prayed Skye would take the hint. She *needed* her twin to make herself scarce this evening, because if things went right, Finn would be there soon.

Skye's identical blue eyes narrowed as she took the shawl. "Why are ye so anxious to get rid of me?"

"Nae reason." Fiona forced her eyes wide and her voice light with innocence. "I just ken how much ye care for the animal, and I ken ye've been down there to check on it—"

"*He* is no' an *it*." Skye frowned, balling the shawl in her fist. "And I thought I'd stay in and keep ye company tonight. I've left ye alone much too often since we arrived at Oliphant Castle."

Nay! Fiona couldn't afford Skye to get protective *now*. "Dinnae be silly. I've enjoyed my time here, meeting new friends. Finn's introduced me to his charming family. They'll be my family soon too."

Tossing the shawl over the back of a chair, Skye grumbled something, which sounded like, "*We'll see.*"

Fiona's pulse began to thunder in her ears as she glanced out the window at the setting sun. Supper had been a relatively quiet affair, with Finn's brothers and sister teasing one another about their father's edict. She'd sat beside him once more, stealing flirtatious glances as her slippered foot teased his muscular calves.

Toward the end of the meal, he'd even leaned over and whispered, "*Soon, my love,*" into her ear, as he stole a kiss beneath her lobe.

The sensation had caused her to shiver—as she shivered now, remembering it—and had also caused his brothers to tease her.

The only one still not present was Duncan, and Agatha had assured everyone he'd be back soon.

Agatha! Maybe that was the excuse she needed.

Fiona scooped up the shawl and began to fold it. Trying for a nonchalant tone, she asked, "Have ye spent any time with Aunt Agatha? She's so delightful. If ye dinnae want to check on yer gelding, ye could go down to the hall and chat with her. She told me she'd be there until late."

Hopefully *late* enough, so Finn could come to the room while Skye was gone.

Her sister had her arms crossed in front of her chest. "*Delightful?*" She snorted. "The daft woman asked if I've heard the mysterious drummer, and when I refused to answer her, kept hounding me. What does it matter if I've heard the annoying prat anyhow? She's mad."

Thinking of the dear old woman's revelation that afternoon, when Fiona shared her decision with Finn in the courtyard, Fiona's lips curled upward slightly. "She might be mad, but there's a method to her madness."

"What?" Skye snapped.

Her sister's tone jerked Fiona's attention from the folded shawl in her hands. "*What?*" She shook her head. "What?"

It was easy to tell that Skye's smile was almost reluctant, as she shook her head. "Ye sound like a mummer, repeating me like that. But I was asking about that phrase ye just spoke. It sounded poetic. Like something a playwright might pen."

Fiona shrugged, getting irritated her sister simply *wouldn't leave.* She tossed the shawl atop their trunk. "Then write it down so that future generations may ken of my brilliance. Mayhap 'twill be spoken in front of kings and queens and multitudes of audiences."

"*Ye're* mad. I only complimented yer turn of phrase."

Fiona sniffed. "And *I* only commanded ye to write it down." Desperate now, she raised her brows hopefully. "There's parchment in the solar."

Skye groaned and rolled her eyes, planting her fists on her hips. "Ye only want me out of here so ye can meet with Finn again, aye? As if 'twas nae bad enough he came in here once and seduced ye."

Fiona gasped, her head jerking back. "*First* of all"—she waggled one finger at her sister—"*I* invited him here that night." Taking a step toward her twin, she waved the finger under Skye's nose. "And *second* of all…"

Damn. What had she been intending to say?

Skye blandly raised a brow in challenge. "Aye?" she drawled.

Planting her hands on her hips, Fiona scowled at her sister.

"Second of all, ye can just go to hell, Skye MacIan! Who are *ye* to judge *me*, just because I want to experience my betrothed's body? I'm going to marry him!"

Skye held up her hands, palms out, but didn't back down. "*Are* ye going to marry him? Do ye *really* ken him?"

Fiona stomped her foot. "*Aye!* I ken him well! *I love him!*"

To her surprise, her twin looked more than a little uncomfortable as she dropped her hands and took a step back, Skye wasn't meeting her eyes, and for the first time since arriving at Oliphant Castle, Fiona thought to wonder exactly how her sister had been spending her days.

But at that moment, she didn't care.

Finn was going to be there any moment, and he was going to make her *his*.

After their kiss in the courtyard, after the way he touched her all throughout supper, she could no longer doubt the fact he wanted her. Somehow, he loved *her*, and wanted *her*, and she wanted *him*!

"Fiona, I think I should tell ye—"

"Nay," Fiona snapped. "Ye dinnae need to tell me aught. I love him, and I will be his wife, so what does it matter if I want him—

Skye clucked her tongue. "I *ken* it! He's coming here tonight, is he no'? 'Tis why ye want me gone."

Sighing, Fiona pinched the bridge of her nose.

Anything to get rid of her.

"Aye, Finn is coming to visit me. But just to talk," she fibbed bravely

Skye's eyes narrowed. "Just to talk? He only wants to talk to ye?"

Swallowing her wince at the lie, Fiona nodded. "Just to talk."

"Aright." Throwing up her hands in defeat, her twin stalked toward the door. "The two of ye have much to talk about, I ken. I'll leave ye to it."

But the look she shot Fiona, right before she pulled the door shut, had Fee wondering what her sister knew.

And why would knowing the truth make Skye seem so stand-offish around Finn?

Frowning again, Fiona turned away from the door and placed her fingertips against her lips. Did they still tingle? That thought led to another, and by the time she'd crossed the room again, she'd forgotten to be irritated with her sister, because she was remembering the feel of Finn's arms around her.

And the feel of his hands *on* her.

In her.

And now that she'd committed herself to him, she'd soon be able to feel *more* of that pleasure and joy.

The sound at the door—not quite a knock—had her whirling around. Before she could call out, it cracked open.

Finn, holding his boots and his sword—so he wouldn't make noise?—slipped through.

She froze, her breath in her throat now that the moment was here. Now that *he* was here.

Moving with a certainty she herself didn't feel, Finn barred the door behind him, then stood his sword against the wall with his boots beside them.

Then he was walking toward her, reaching for her, holding her.

Then he was kissing her, and everything was wonderful.

But somehow, through the bliss of having him in her arms, through the sensations his lips were dragging from her, she remembered her promise to her sister. There was a way to make it *not* a lie, right?

"Wait," she gasped, pushing away from him. "We have to…"

It was the way he was looking at her—like he wanted to consume her—which had her trailing off, forgetting her words. Her hands rose to his chest, marveling at the warmth and firmness she found there. Humming, she brushed her palms against the pebbles of his nipples, then across his shoulders and down his finely muscled arms.

"Fiona?" he murmured.

"Hmm?" *By all the saints in Heaven, who knew a man's forearms could make my knees so weak?*

"Ye were saying we have to do something?"

What *had* she been saying? "Oh, aye!" she blurted. "We have to talk."

When had his hands settled on her hips? "Talk? About what?"

She shrugged, her attention now on the intriguing spot at the base of his throat. It was a sort of divot, and Fiona realized she was already leaning forward, ready to taste it.

But he'd asked her a question, hadn't he?

"I dinnae ken," she whispered, her breath against his skin. "I promised Skye ye were coming here to talk…" She paused to brush a kiss on that fascinating spot, and loved his unique, salty taste. "So we have to talk."

Finn dropped his head back with a groan, exposing more of his neck to her lips. "What should we talk about?"

Talking? He wanted to *talk* at a time like this?

Fiona ran her hands down his side, her palms encountering his belt, before she skipped to his kilt. There was a delicious *something* pressing against her belly just *there*, and she needed to touch it.

Sliding her hands beneath his kilt, she wrapped her fingers

around the firm length of him, then smiled when she heard him suck in a breath.

"I think we should talk about *this*," she said impishly, suddenly very bold.

"Ye—ye want to talk about my *cock*?" he choked out.

"Yer cock," she repeated, trying out the sound of the word on her tongue as she straightened to grin at him. "*Cock*." She hummed. "Aye, I suspect 'twill be one of my favorite topics, once we're married."

The look in his eyes seemed to be somewhere between joy and desperation. "As long as ye only discuss it with *me*, Fiona."

Speculatively, she stroked his shaft with one hand, while reaching to explore *more* of him with the other. He made an odd sort of noise, then swallowed.

"Ye're sure about this, Fee? Ye mean to be my wife?"

She stilled, one hand cupping his bollocks—and *how* she wished this marvelous tool wasn't hidden by his kilt!

"Aye," she whispered, meeting his eyes. "I've realized something today." Thanks to his mother, not that he needed to know that.

"That I love ye? Ye finally understand that?"

She shook her head. "I've realized the fact ye are *committed* to me is even more valuable. We're going to fight, I ken it. And there will likely be a time when I dinnae feel this same overwhelming desire every time I look at ye. But I love ye, and ye love me, and that commitment is what matters."

His tongue darted out over his lower lip. "And what about building a sound foundation of shared memories?"

Oh, he was teasing her, was he? Two could play that game.

Smiling slyly, she twitched her fingers, the pad of her thumb brushing against the tip of his still-stiff member.

"Remember the first night ye made me yers? I fondled yer cock, felt it grow in my hands, salivated at the thought of it in me?"

His eyes went wide, and when he spoke, he sounded as if he were being strangled. "I do remember that. I almost spent myself in yer palm, so I think we should…"

Instead of finishing his thought, Finn tried to step back, to pull out of her hold.

"Nay!" Her hands tightened around him and he stilled instantly. "Nay," she repeated softer. "I havenae had my fill of ye." Her tone turned mischievous as she began to stroke him again. "But when it comes to memories, I recall being disappointed I couldnae *see* what I was getting."

"Fee..." he managed, though in a hoarse whisper.

And that fierce *pride*—the idea she could reduce a strong man like this to such desperation—had her dropping his cock and reaching for his belt.

Finn didn't try to stop her, and soon, he was standing nude before her.

Stepping back, she dragged her gaze down his magnificent body, feeling bloody powerful to be examining him like this while she was still fully dressed.

Her gaze was drawn inexorably to his *cock*, standing stiff and straight from its bed of wiry curls, which was a few shades darker than the hair on his head.

She licked her lips.

"Stop looking at me like I'm a ham hock ye want to devour," he whispered, part command and part plea.

She smirked, her eyes darting to his, before dropping once more. "I was thinking more of a sausage. A nice, thick, hard, *juicy* sausage."

With a groan and a roll of his eyes, Finn launched into motion, reaching out and grabbing her. The kiss he dropped to her lips was fast and hard, and she got the impression he was just trying to shut her up.

When he pulled back, his lips tugged up wryly at one side.

"Will ye always make stupid jokes in my bed?"

Still feeling bold, Fiona shrugged. "I dinnae ken," she said impishly. "I'm no' in yer bed yet."

"Let us rectify that," he growled.

When he scooped her up, she squealed and clung to him...but

only for as long as it took him to deposit her on *his* bed—the one she'd been sleeping in these last several days.

She opened her mouth to point that out to him, but then sucked in a surprised breath when his lips went to the base of her neck. His hands were on her—gentle, then firm, caressing, *yearning*—roaming over her breasts and hips and gown.

Then her gown was gone, and her chemise and stockings as well, and all she could focus on was the glorious, maddening sensations his hands wrought upon her.

Then his fingers were *there*, burrowing in her curls, as his mouth closed around one of her nipples. It was *so* much better than when he'd kissed her through her chemise, because now, she could feel his whiskers against her sensitive skin, and the sensation drove her wild.

"Finn!" she begged, not completely sure *what* she was pleading for.

"Aye, lass," he whispered against her skin, his lips trailing over her breast, "tell me."

She arched her back under his caresses. "I want—I want to touch ye. I want to explore ye."

'Tis what she'd set out to do that evening, after all.

In a flash, he peeled himself off her, flattening himself beside her on the bed. With his full body on display, his cock jutting upward, all straight and proud.

"Explore all ye want, my love," Finn growled.

Suddenly shy, Fiona pushed herself upright, unable to deny her curiosity. He was magnificent, splayed out as he was, simply to assuage her curiosity.

As she skimmed a light touch down his flank, his hands curled into fists around the coverlets at his side, but that was the only indication he gave to show he was affected. When she stole a glance at him, nibbling on her bottom lip, he was watching her.

The fact he hadn't tried to stop her—the fact he was *offering* himself like this—made her feel bolder.

Her fingers skimmed across his thighs, then over his curls. He jerked just slightly when she cupped his bollocks again, feeling their weight against her palm, as she experimented with his stiff member. She wrapped one thumb and forefinger around it, marveling at the way it felt like velvet...velvet wrapped around steel.

His cock had a freckle, a large one, right on the tip. It was impossible to look away from.

Slowly, she dragged her hand up his shaft, then down again. His breath hissed between his lips, but she couldn't pull her gaze away from her work to see his reaction. It was *fascinating* to realize *she'd* been the one to cause this magnificent member to stiffen.

A bead of moisture had gathered at the tip, and her lips parted, breathless. She *knew* what this meant, of course, but *seeing* it was different from *hearing* about a man's desires and pleasures.

That ache was back, deep in her core, and she shifted on the bed, desperate for relief. The movement brought her closer to *him*, her eyes transfixed on that freckle at the tip of his cock.

What would it taste like?

Salty, like his skin?

Or sweet, like his love?

She was leaning closer, lips parted farther, when he grabbed her elbow.

"*Fiona*," he growled. "If ye do that, I'll no' be able to make ye mine."

When she straightened and glanced up at him, he was breathing heavily.

"I want to be *inside* ye, love."

The thought of not being able to taste him was disappointing, but she couldn't deny the surge of heat at his words. *Another time*, she promised herself.

"I want that too," she whispered.

His nod was brief, aye, but she felt as if he were giving her a blessing. He released her arm, then rested his head back on the mattress.

Taking a deep breath, she threw one leg over his thighs, until she was straddling his hips. Her curls cradled his stiff member, and as she pressed herself forward, his firmness made her aware of just how *wet* she was.

Experimentally, she leaned toward his chest, dragging her damp slit along his cock. The friction was delightful, made even better by the strangled noise he made. When she did it again, his fingers dug into the coverlets by his side, his jaw clenched as he breathed deeply, deliberately.

"Is this aright, Finn?"

"Aright?" he repeated hoarsely, his eyes honest. "If it were any better, I'd be dead, lass."

His admission made her smile, and she *knew* she was ready.

And because he'd given her the power, she could be the one to make that decision.

So she shifted herself up and over his cock, then slowly sat back. She lowered herself around him, each inch bringing a tightness and burn she hadn't expected. She'd known there would be pain, but *this* was—

"Breathe, lass."

It wasn't until she opened her eyes that she realized she'd closed them. She was stiff, frozen, her muscles clenched as her entire being focused on the throbbing in her core.

But there was concern in his gaze. "Fee, just breathe."

When his fingers skimmed over her knee, then her thigh, she exhaled.

"It'll be aright, love. I swear it."

His touches continued, feather-light, across her thighs. She inhaled. Then exhaled again.

And felt her muscles slowly loosen.

This is *aright.*

As she relaxed against him—*atop* him—she found it was easier to breathe. And somehow, the pain wasn't quite so intense. In fact, the throbbing seemed to be centered differently now, causing her to want to *move.*

His touches continued up her side to her breasts, and they felt wonderful.

Sighing, she arched into his touch as his thumbs circled her nipples, and the movement caused his member to shift inside her.

That felt even *better*.

With wide eyes, she did it again, just the slightest little rocking motion, and released a breathless whimper.

Saints be praised, that felt *wonderful*.

By the fourth time she rocked back and forth atop his cock, she realized he'd frozen, his hands on her breasts. Glancing down, she realized the muscles of his jaw had gone tight, and he appeared to be in pain.

Worried now, she halted her movement. "Does that feel aright?"

With a strangled whisper, he admitted, "It feels as if I've died and gone to heaven. Dinnae stop."

She bit her lip. "Then why do ye look as if—

"Because I'm trying to keep from taking command," he growled. "I've waited for this for months, but tonight is about *ye*."

It was sweet.

It was *stupid*.

"The last time ye came to me in this room, Finn Oliphant, ye gave me pleasure. Tonight, I want us *both* to find pleasure."

He didn't even argue. Just growled an, "Aye" and bucked his hips slightly, driving his swollen member deeper inside and causing her to suck in a gasp at the sensation.

It had felt good to move atop him, but it felt even *better* for him to move in *her*.

So she leaned forward, placing her palms against the mattress on either side of his shoulders, and met his eyes. "Do that again," she commanded.

And he did.

Oh.

Oh my.

As Fiona braced her knees on either side of his hips and took her weight on her palms, Finn slid in and out of her in the most delicious tempo. She swallowed, arching her pelvis into him, to create even more friction, as he grasped her hips with a guttural groan.

They were both panting, and she could feel herself coming apart at the edges, like a frayed cloth pulled too hard.

"Finn!" she gasped, not sure what she was asking.

He didn't stop, but pressed up into her so hard, she moaned.

"Finn! *Now*! Please!"

And miracle of miracles, he understood her gasping plea.

With a guttural roar, he flipped her over. She had no idea how it happened, except one moment she was staring down at him, and the next she was on her back, his hands grasping her knees, and his cock slamming into her once more. The sensation was so powerful, so wonderful, her arse came up off the bed as she planted her heels and offered herself to his pleasure.

But he leaned forward, mimicking her pose from a moment before, and the pressure of him against the sensitive spot above her wetness caused white flashes behind her eyes.

She realized she was holding her breath, but couldn't seem to make herself release the muscles to force her lungs to work. All she knew was that she…was…*almost*…there.

Then, his breaths coming in pants, he reached between them to the place where they were joined, and dragged one callused thumb across the center of her pleasure.

Her climax burst upon her, every part of her body tightening around him, squeezing him closer. The sensation must have coaxed him, because he called her name as he threw his head back, and a flood of warmth spilled against her womb.

That knowledge—or mayhap the way he continued to leisurely stroke in and out of her—prolonged her pleasure.

But much too short a time later, the two of them collapsed, spent and panting, in one another's arms.

It was *everything*.

Finn took the time to untangle himself, then slipped away to dip a rag in the bowl of water near the window. When he climbed back in bed, he lovingly cleaned her, pausing when the evidence of her virginity came away on the cloth.

His fierce look of pride as he spotted those drops of blood had her flushing—partly from embarrassment, partly from remembered pleasure.

But then he tossed the rag aside, pulled down the coverlet, took her in his arms, and wrapped them both under the blanket. As they cuddled there beneath the linen, her cheek and ear pressed against his chest, and his chin resting atop her head, Fiona felt herself smile.

For the first time since she'd met Finn, all her doubts were gone.

She loved him, and he loved her. They would marry and be able to do this many more times.

Her smile grew as his heart beat under her skin.

This was *perfect*.

CHAPTER 10

FINN AWOKE BEFORE DAWN, the familiar surroundings now feeling *different*.

Mayhap 'twas because of the naked angel in his arms. Or mayhap *he* was different.

He was going to be married and couldn't be happier.

Last night, he'd finally made Fiona his, and their joining had been as perfect as he'd expected. After they'd both recovered from their first time, he'd set about showing her some of the ways a man and a woman could bring one another pleasure, and he didn't think he'd *ever* forget the way her climax had exploded over his tongue when he'd used his mouth on her.

But now…?

Now she slept soundly, curled on her side like a kitten. He imagined he could hear her purring in satisfaction, being well-pleased and well-loved.

And as for him?

Well, he'd be even happier once she was his wife.

For now though, it likely wouldn't do for someone—someone like her sister—to discover them in bed before the ceremony. So, reluctantly, Finn slid from the bed, but not before leaning over to place a light kiss on her cheek.

Fiona didn't stir.

He made short work of folding and belting on his plaid, then gathering up his things. He *did* take the time to pull on his boots and strap on his scabbard, so if any of his family found him sneaking around the corridors before the rest of the keep was awake, they wouldn't guess what he'd been doing.

Actually, if it were his *brothers* who caught him, they'd likely guess after just one look at the satisfaction in his eyes.

But he wasn't going to bother denying it. Fiona was now *his*, in every way but marriage. Surprisingly, over the last few days he'd spent frantically trying to convince her to agree to be his wife, Finn hadn't been thinking of Da's ultimatum. The idea of Fee carrying his child, of giving him sons, wasn't as appealing, because it would mean becoming laird.

Nay, Finn had realized something important: laird or not, it was the building of a life with Fiona by his side which mattered. He wanted her for *her*, not for the position or power she might bring him by birthing a son.

He loved her, and she loved him, and that was that.

No one else was usually awake at this hour, so he was surprised to step into the great hall and see a figure sitting at the high table. With the sky still dark outside the windows, it was hard to tell who it was, but Finn had a hunch...

As he got closer, he realized he was right. His twin brother Duncan sat hunched in the semi-darkness, fiddling with the bowl of porridge in front of him.

"Welcome home, brother," Finn said in a low voice as he slid onto the stool across from Duncan.

His twin was mid-bite, but even that couldn't hide the irritated pull of his brows. Finn knew his brother would be frowning, if he weren't eating.

"What are ye—"

Finn bit off his words when an eerie pounding drifted through the wall closest to them. Both brothers turned to scowl at the stone, as if it personally were at fault.

" 'Tis impossible to tell if 'tis the drummer, or the English come back to make trouble for us," Finn muttered.

"By St. Simon's left nostril, this shite is getting ridiculous," Duncan growled in response. " 'Tis getting where a man cannae *sleep*."

Is that why Dunc looked so irritated?

His rest had been interrupted by the drummer, who apparently doomed men to fall in love?

Ignoring his growling stomach—and the ghostly rhythm, which was now moving off to bother another section of the keep—Finn planted his elbows on the table and laced his fingers together.

"Have ye heard him all night?"

Duncan shrugged, scooping up another bite of porridge. "I just got back. Headed to the kitchens for something to break my fast with."

Hmm. So if he hadn't been here all night, then that meant Duncan had heard the Drummer of Oliphant Castle *prior* to his trip. And if Aunt Agatha's theory was correct, then *he* was *dooooooomed* to fall in love as well.

Finn's lips twitched, wondering if his brother was scowling now because of whatever woman had captured his heart.

But as he watched Duncan shovel another large spoonful of the honey-sweetened porridge into his mouth, Finn's stomach growled loudly. When his twin glanced up at him, Finn grinned sheepishly and shrugged.

"I have an appetite this morning," he offered as an excuse.

Duncan looked as if he wanted to say something—was he going to question *where* Finn had been all evening?—but at that moment, Moira appeared at Finn's elbow.

"Good morning, Finn," she said with a soft smile, as she placed a bowl of porridge before him. "I thought ye might be hungry."

Catching the older woman's hand, he brought it to his lips for a grateful kiss. "Ye're a goddess, Moira. Ye needn't wait on the likes of me though. Why are ye even awake at this hour?"

To his surprise, the housekeeper blushed. The sunrise offered just enough light to make out the way her cheeks darkened as she lifted her free hand to pat at her bun. Come to think of it, her hair was in disarray, as if she'd just come from bed.

The older woman stammered something about seeing to the kitchens and hurried off.

Finn met his twin's gaze with a raised brow, but Dunc just shrugged and went back to his breakfast. Finn joined him until his hunger was satiated, and he felt his energy returning from his night of loving Fiona.

"So just got home, eh?" Duncan grunted in agreement. "So why are ye looking like a frog in the garderobe? Did ye no' get to Larg in time for yer Master?"

Dunc sighed and tossed his spoon into his now-empty bowl. "Nay, I got there, and Master Claire's health is improving each day. I stayed in order to help with a few commissions. But now the Master is sending me to Eriboll to pick up some of her completed works."

"Why?" St. Ninian's knees, but this porridge was good!

His twin scowled. "One of the Master's clients has died, and his widow needs funds. She offered Claire the chance to buy back the pieces—mainly jewelry—which the man had commissioned. So I get the duty of traveling to purchase them back."

"And ye dinnae want to bother with the trip?" Finn shrugged, answering his own question. "But 'tis logical ye be the one to go; ye are skilled with a sword, even if ye dinnae care to use one, and ye can recognize the pieces to make sure there's nae cheating."

"Aye," Duncan grumbled, crossing his arms in front of his chest.

In the growing light, Finn narrowed his eyes as he examined his twin's mood. "Unless…'tis no' the journey which has ye looking as if ye swallowed bannock dry."

His twin blew out a loud breath. " 'Tis a *woman*, of course."

"Of course," Finn murmured, hiding his smile behind a spoonful of breakfast.

But one of Dunc's hands slammed down on the wooden table-top. "Ye dinnae need to smirk, ye ken, just because *ye've* had luck with a lady."

"Hold!" Finn pointed his spoon at his brother's nose. " 'Twas no' so simple as to be dismissed. It has taken me every day since ye left to convince her to go through with marrying me. I eventually had to go to Mam and urge her to talk to Fiona on my behalf."

Duncan snorted. "Poor ye." He waved toward Finn's face. "A blind man could see from yer stupid grin ye've overcome her objections."

"Stupid grin?"

"Ye look well and truly satisfied."

Finn shrugged, knowing he was still smiling. "I like to think I satisfied *her*."

When his brother snorted again and folded his arms, Finn leaned forward. "Are ye going to tell me what *woman* has ye acting so prickly?"

For a long moment, he wasn't sure Duncan would agree. Finally, his twin shrugged his shoulders and tipped his head back, his hair—the same shade and length as Finn's—falling across the back of his chair.

"As I was saddling my horse to leave Oliphant Castle, a pretty lass came into the stables." Duncan's eyes closed, one corner of his lips twitching upright in that wry way he had. "She kenned a lot about horses, and we discussed her gelding—an animal almost as pretty and as feisty as she."

"Ye dinnae ken the lass?"

Dunc shrugged. "I assumed she was with the MacIan party, but…"

When he trailed off, Finn dropped his spoon into his bowl. "Aye?" he prompted.

His brother's eyes opened, and he looked a little sheepish when he admitted, "Neither of us thought to ask the other's name."

"Because ye were *busy*, I assume?"

Now his grin grew. "Aye, ye could say that. Her kiss was as powerful as the rest of her."

Finn could just imagine it. His brother—normally taciturn and happy to be left alone—had likely gotten into a disagreement with the *pretty lass*. One thing led to another, and once the kissing had started, they both likely stopped thinking.

He jumped to conclusions. "So ye're scowling now, because ye cannae find her to wet yer wick again?"

Duncan pushed himself upright, his grin fading once more. "It went nae further than kissing, afore she ran off. But this morn, when I returned to stable my horse, I saw her again."

"Really?" Finn frowned, wondering who this lass could be. "In the stables?"

"Aye, sleeping in the hay. She looked so damn angelic, I couldnae help myself."

Finn felt his lips twitching at his brother's expense. "Ye kissed her."

It wasn't a question, but Duncan concurred. "I kissed her."

"And she didnae like being taken advantage of like that."

"She punches like a man."

When Dunc lifted his fingertips to his left cheekbone, Finn stopped trying to hold in his chuckles.

With a growl, his twin brother lunged across the table at him. Startled, Finn jerked out of the way, only to topple backward off his stool.

His ego hurt more than his arse, but he still took his time getting up, only to discover Duncan's mood much improved. His brother was smiling now, and Finn joined him.

"Come on, Dunc." He beckoned toward the main doors. "Let us go see if Mam's awake." He wanted to ask if she'd spoken with Fiona yesterday—if his mother was the reason his love had changed her mind—and older woman could likely offer Duncan some advice as well.

"I've told ye no' to call me that." Duncan growled again as he pushed himself to his feet.

Finn shrugged, already backing toward the doors. "I'll stop, when ye *make* me stop."

"Fook ye."

It was all the warning Finn got, before Duncan broke into a run. With a yelp, Finn turned and ran toward the door.

When they reached the gates on the other side of the courtyard, Finn was still in the lead, just out of his brother's reach...and both were laughing.

FIONA WOKE when the door opened.

She stretched languidly, a soft grin on her face, as her muscles protested to the disturbance. She wanted to lie there, basking in the glory which was her body. Now that Finn had made her realize exactly how powerful and desirable she really was—

Finn!

Her chest clenched when she realized he wasn't in bed with her, and she wasn't sure if she was pleased, or disappointed. It would be wonderful to wake up beside him, but she supposed they would have years to learn about each other's morning routines.

Besides, it would be difficult to explain what he was doing in her bed if a servant were to discover them together like this, just as dawn was breaking.

"Are ye awake?"

A servant...or her *sister*.

Where had Skye been all this time?

Fiona admitted to herself she'd completely forgotten about her twin once Finn had started touching her. Thank the saints her sister had decided to stay away all evening, and thank the saints Finn had snuck out before she'd returned.

"Ye *are* awake, I can tell. Why are ye pretending?"

With a sigh, Fiona pushed back the coverlet to glare at her sister, who stood at the foot of the bed with her arms crossed and her foot tapping. She looked extremely put out, and her foot was tapping more impatiently by the second.

Fiona noticed her sister's braid was disheveled, and there was hay in her hair.

Trying to put Skye on the defensive, Fiona frowned. "Where have ye been? And why do ye look as if ye've slept in the stables?"

That was apparently the wrong thing to ask, judging by the way Skye's scowl darkened.

"Because I *did* sleep in the stables. Why are ye naked?"

Oh, damn. Fee had forgotten that little fact when she'd sat up, and now she pulled the coverlet up higher as she shrugged nonchalantly. " 'Twas a warm night."

Skye snorted and whirled away, stomping toward the window to shut it. "Did ye have yer *talk* with Finn?" she called mockingly over her shoulder.

"Aye." Fiona shifted on the mattress, inching toward the edge of the bed, and wondering if she could reach her gown.

"And ye just talked?"

Reaching the edge of the bed, Fee leaned down, stretching for her chemise, while also trying to keep the coverlet covering her breasts. Instead of lying directly to her sister, she hummed, as if distracted.

From the incredulous noise Skye made, she obviously wasn't buying it.

The damn chemise was just out of reach. With a frustrated grunt, Fiona gave up on her modesty—after all, it wasn't as if Skye had never seen her nude before—snatched up the under gown, and pulled herself upright in bed once more, all the while fumbling to get the thing over her head.

When she emerged from the linen, proud she'd avoided the question, Skye was still staring at her. But this time, her expression was incredulous. It was only then that Fiona glanced around her, seeing the rumpled bedclothes, the indention of two bodies...and the incriminating speckles of blood.

She flushed.

"He wasnae here all night," Fiona hastened to assure her sister, as if it would make a difference.

At least 'tis no' a lie. I dinnae ken when he left.

But her twin's frown didn't ease. In fact, it got worse, her nose wrinkling, as if she'd eaten something rancid.

"Oh, I *ken* he wasnae here all night," Skye muttered, her angry gaze dropping to the foot of the bed.

Why did she look as if she wanted to personally chop the thing into firewood?

Or was her scowl for something else?

For *Finn*?

"Skye…"

She wasn't sure what she'd been intending to say. Not to apologize for her actions, that was for certain. She loved Finn, and he loved her, and what did it *matter* if they anticipated their vows?

But whatever her intentions were, they were dashed when her twin's chin jerked up and she dropped her hands to her hips, in that take-command way she had.

"Did ye have sex with him, Fee?"

Fiona reared back in surprise. "What?"

"Och, I'm sorry," her twin said sarcastically. Then she gave an elaborate bow, her hands twirling on her wrists as if she were a courtier being presented to the Pope. "Last eventide, did ye grant yer charming lover yer maidenhead, in a physical manifestation of yer love for one another?"

"*What?*"

Skye straightened. Enunciating her words as if Fiona was hard of hearing, she said loudly, "Did. Ye. Fook. Him?"

Fiona didn't answer.

She didn't *have* to answer.

Her blush did the answering. It told Skye all she needed to know. In fact, it likely *screamed* it from the battlements.

With a groan, Skye twisted away, tugging at the tie on the end of her braid. "*Feeeeee!*"

Fiona had always hated the way her twin could drag out her nickname like that. "What?" she asked, yet again, as she swung her legs over the edge of the bed and sat up. "What does it matter? I'm going to marry the man!"

"*Are ye sure?*" her sister hissed, not turning back to look at her.

"Of *course* I'm sure! I made my decision yesterday!" Fiona threw up her hands. "Why are ye being so—so—so *difficult?*" Skye had been like this last night too, now that she thought about it. "Do ye no' *want* me to be happy?"

Her sister's shoulders slumped, halfway through pulling her hair out of the braid. The brown curls, identical to Fiona's, swung trapped halfway down her back, hay sticking out at weird angles.

"I'm afraid for ye, Fee," Skye whispered. "I'm afraid ye dinnae ken him well enough."

The words were ridiculous, but Fiona's heart broke for the fear in her sister's voice. "Oh, Skye." She rushed across the room and took her sister's shoulders. " 'Tis no' like that. I ken, at one point, I was terrified he dinnae want me for *me.* But in the last few days, being with him, *learning about him,* I've discovered Finn Oliphant is a wonderful man, and I want naught more than to be his wife."

Slowly, Skye turned, her blue eyes worried, as she took Fiona's hands. "Before we arrived, ye were concerned ye were no' worthy of his love."

Fee smiled softly. " 'Twas before he convinced me I *am* worthy—worthy of so much!"

"But *he* is no' worth of *yer* love, Fee. I'm sorry." Squeezing her hands, Skye's eyes darted between her sister's. "I dinnae want to hurt ye, but ye cannae give him yer heart, *or* yer hand."

Too late.

Fiona shook her head, trying to understand why her sister would say such a thing.

Skye nodded.

Fiona shook her head again.

Skye nodded *again.*

"Skye! Dinnae tease me about something like this."

"I would never."

Fiona tried to pull her hands away, but her sister wouldn't let them go. "Why would ye say something so horrible about Finn? I love him, and I *will* marry him!"

"He doesnae love *ye*, Fiona."

This time, she succeeded in jerking her hands out of Skye's hold, and Fiona stumbled back, still shaking her head.

And Skye—*damn her!*—nodded solemnly for a third time.

"The night we arrived, Fee, he kissed me in the stables."

Gasping, Fiona's hand covered her lips, remembering Finn's greeting. He'd reached for *Skye* first, because her sister was the prettier of the two. He'd reached for Skye, to kiss her, because next to her twin, Fiona wasn't worthy.

"I'm so sorry," her sister whispered, her eyes full of pain, "but I kissed him back. He *is* a bonny man, after all."

Fiona's eyes filled with tears. "How could ye?"

Her sister wrapped her arms around her stomach, shrinking in upon herself. "After the way he reached for *me* when we arrived, I thought he was naught more than a harmless charmer. And ye'd just been saying how ye werenae sure ye'd marry him. I thought some flirting wouldnae be amiss…" Skye's lips quavered. "And when he kissed me, I was so surprised, I went along with it, before I regained my wits." She sucked in a breath. "I swear to ye, as soon as I realized what I was doing, I pulled away. But *he* dinnae seem ashamed, as he ought to have been."

Fiona was shaking, but she wasn't sure if it was in anger or shock, and she lifted her other hand to her mouth.

Finn had kissed her sister?

Their first evening here on Oliphant land.

The same evening he came to yer room and made ye scream his name.

He *was* a flirt, a charmer. 'Twas one of the things she loved about him.

Mayhap he'd just been trying to charm Skye to get to her?

If kissing is part of his charm, then he's likely kissed a good many lasses.

He'd kissed her in Wick last autumn, hadn't he?

Aye.

And kissed her any number of times since she'd arrived here at Oliphant Castle.

Aye.

He'd kissed Skye...on the very same night he'd come to her bed.

Her chest tight, Fiona met her sister's eyes, and saw the worry in them. Somehow, she knew this wasn't the worst of it.

"Fee..."

Fiona curled her hands into fists in front of her lips. "Just tell me," she managed to say.

Skye winced. "I...I slept in the stable last night. I hadnae intended to, just fell asleep there. And this morning..."

This morning.

"Aye?" she whispered hoarsely.

Her twin met her eyes. "This morning, I awoke to his kiss. His lips were on mine, his hands on my body, and I punched him for it."

Lips on mine, hands on my body.

An iciness crept over Fiona. She dropped her hands and straightened her back.

Finn had crawled from her bed this morning after taking her virginity, and went straight to Skye.

And Skye, knowing now how Fiona felt about him, had punched him.

Her own hands curled into fists again, and she realized she was ready to punch him too.

"How could he?" she whispered.

Skye shook her head, the movement causing her hair to fall completely from its braid. "Ye had a feeling this marriage wouldnae be a strong one, Fee. 'Tis obvious from the start he doesnae intend to be faithful to ye."

Despite what he claimed.

"Mayhap 'tis possible to hold a man's heart, but no' his fidelity," Fiona murmured thoughtfully, her gaze locked on the far wall.

"I'm sorry." Skye stepped up beside her, pulling her into an embrace. "I'm so sorry. If I'd kenned how ye felt about him, I never would've returned that kiss the night we arrived. I wasnae thinking straight, I suppose."

Fiona just hummed, dropping her cheek to her twin's shoulder.

She ached all over.

Her eyes ached from holding back the tears. Her core ached from the horrible, wonderful, *life-changing* things Finn had shown her last night.

And her heart…?

Her heart ached most of all.

"Mayhap 'tis better to ken this now?" Skye whispered, holding her tightly. "Afore the wedding ceremony?"

Wedding ceremony!

Stewart had given them until *today* to decide if she would marry Finn Oliphant. Well, all she had to do was march down to the great hall and explain to her brother, *Thank ye, but nay*, she'd be returning to the MacIan keep. To her old life.

She sniffed. "At least I'll get to see Allison's bairn, and hold our wee niece or nephew."

Skye snorted in return. "Dinnae pretend yer heart isnae breaking, Fee. I ken ye."

Aye, the same way she'd thought she'd known Finn.

Squeezing her eyes shut, she gave in to despair, allowing the tears to flow unchecked. "I thought I had found my *forever*, Skye. I was going to miss ye so, *so* much."

Her sister rubbed her back. "And I'd gladly take on that pain, Fee, if it meant yer happiness. But I *had* to tell ye. I couldnae allow Stewart to leave ye here, married to Finn, kenning the man is unfaithful."

And with her own sister.

Fiona's arms snaked around Skye's middle, and she cried. She cried for what she'd lost, what she'd given up, and what had been stolen.

CHAPTER 11

It wasn't noon yet, but Finn was feeling…*itchy*, for some reason. He bounced slightly on the balls of his feet, his hands curling and uncurling, as he stood with his twin in the great hall once more and listened to Malcolm discuss politics with Duncan.

Really, was it any wonder Finn's attention was on the stairs?

He hadn't seen Fiona yet this morning. Not since he'd left her in his bed, at least. He'd spent the morning in the village, where Dunc had a long chat with their stepfather about hammer heat, or some such nonsense, then practically flown back up to the keep. He'd been hanging around the hall for almost an hour, wondering at what point he could go wake her up.

He was ready to sign the betrothal contract, but needed her at his side when he did so.

"Ye're no' *still* talking about English politics, are ye?" Kiergan ambled up, Nessa on his arm.

Malcolm sighed. "How will ye learn aught, if ye refuse to listen?"

"I listen to what *matters*."

"Women's moans of pleasure are *no'* the most important thing to listen to," Malcolm said with a roll of his eyes.

"Says ye—"

In an effort to head off the arguing, Finn interrupted, overly loud. "Good morn, Nessa!"

Their sister was looking irritated at something. "Is it?"

Kiergan winced. "Da signed another contract for her."

Duncan groaned. "Henry Campbell isnae yet cold in his grave! Who is it this time?"

"One of the Duffus's sons."

Malcolm's brows drew in. "Henry?"

Nessa sighed. "*Of course.* I cannae tell if Da is going out of his way to find Henrys, or if 'tis just a stroke of fate."

"I hope he survives," Kiergan muttered.

As their sister turned to him, her mouth opened—likely to snap marriage to her was worth more than *surviving*—Finn intervened once more.

Since Finn wasn't sure how in the hell he was going to get out of this conversation, and since Duncan was being zero help, he was grateful when Stewart MacIan strolled up.

That was, until the man got a good look at Duncan standing beside Finn, and interrupted Nessa with a blurted, "Good God, ye're identical."

Then, shaking his head, he turned to Nessa. "I'm sorry for interrupting ye, milady. I'm sure whatever ye were saying was important." He ignored the strangled noise Duncan made. "But I was surprised. I kenned there was still one brother I hadnae met, but— Wait, which one of ye is Finn?"

Before any of them could answer, Finn's attention was caught by the two women coming down the stairs. His heart leapt—'twas Fiona and her sister! At last, Fee would be able to tell Stewart herself she would marry Finn, and they could start their lives together.

At the base of the steps, Aunt Agatha stopped Skye, calling out her name. Fee's twin looked irritated—of course, she *always* looked irritated, as far as Finn could tell—but turned to speak with the old woman.

Fiona stomped toward their group, looking like an angel.

Had she been sleeping all this time, or spending hours dressing?

She looked beautiful in that blue gown, her hair all pinned up, but he preferred her the way he had her last night, naked and—

Why were her eyes red and puffy?

And how come, the closer she got, the easier it was to see the storm clouds in her expression?

"Uh-oh," muttered Stewart, as he hurried toward her.

Fiona stopped short as she reached her brother and crossed her arms in front of her. "Nay!"

"What?" Stewart asked.

"My answer is *nay*. I'll no' marry him."

Finn had *heard* of people's blood running cold, but had never experienced it.

Until that moment.

With just those few words, he felt as if the floor had dropped out from underneath him, and he was falling, falling...falling to hell?

He struggled to suck in a breath, stumbling toward her, not even noticing Duncan following him.

Last night, she'd said she was sure. Said she'd marry him. She wouldn't have let him touch her the way he had—*surely*—if she didn't intend to marry him?

Her brother turned back to Finn and Duncan—and Nessa, who was drifting behind—and frowned. "Why no'?"

Fiona's frown darkened as she followed Stewart's gaze. "Because Finn Oliphant is a— Oh, wait, there's two of him."

"Of *us*," Duncan corrected, unhelpfully.

She shook her head. "Which one of ye is Finn? Oh, it doesnae matter. I assume this is Duncan? Elsa said the two of ye looked alike but—well, nice to meet ye, Duncan, whichever one ye are." Niceties over, she turned back to her brother, her shoulders hunched over her crossed arms. "I'll no' marry Finn Oliphant, because he's a womanizer, a rogue, who uses his charm to seduce women, even while claiming to love another."

Finn's mouth opened, but nothing more than a confused croak

emerged. He was too shocked—and frankly, *hurt*—by her accusations, to say anything more.

It was his twin brother who stepped forward to defend him. "That's no' true," Duncan began.

But Fiona whirled on him. "Ye shut up, Finn!" she snapped. "I *loved* ye. I willingly gave myself to ye, thinking ye loved me in return!"

Duncan shook his head. "If Finn said he loved ye—"

Her foot slammed into the floor. "Dinnae try to weasel out of this! Ye've told me time and again ye loved me, only to leave my bed and go paw at my sister. *My sister!*"

Finn made that same strangled, shocked noise again—a denial, but no one could tell—as Duncan looked confused as hell. What did Fiona mean, accusing him of *pawing* at her sister, or seducing another woman? Finn had never done those things—never even *thought* of doing those things—and as soon as he could make his voice work, he'd explain.

But then Stewart took control of the conversation. "Ye've lain with this man?" he asked in a deceptively quiet voice. "Ye're nae longer a virgin?"

Mayhap Fiona could see how furious her brother was, at the admission she and Finn had anticipated their vows a bit, because her frown grew mulish, and she gave her brother her shoulder. "It matters naught. Ye cannae force me to marry him."

Before Stewart could answer—could explain that, aye, he *could* force her to marry Finn—Skye hurried up to their group. "I'm glad *that's* over."

Beside him, Duncan muttered, "St. Simon's uvula, they're *twins*? Yer betrothed has an identical *twin*?"

Skye obviously hadn't heard, because she was still ranting about her delay, caused by Aunt Agatha. "She thought it *vital* to ken if I'd heard drumming last night." Skye rolled her eyes. "Of *course* I heard the drumming. The whole damn keep heard the drumming."

Nessa lifted one finger. "I didnae."

"Anyhow, sorry." Skye shrugged. "But I'm here now to support ye, Fee, against this— Oh shite! There's *two* of them?"

The last was blurted when she finally got a good look at Duncan, but Fiona waved away her confusion with her angry explanation. "Apparently they're twins. Identical twins, just like ye and me," she snapped.

But Finn met Skye's gaze and saw doubt creep across those familiar blue eyes, as she looked from him to Duncan and back again.

How much was *she* to blame for Fiona's words now?

But Stewart refused to be dismissed. "Fiona, if ye've given yerself to Finn Oliphant, then ye're as good as married, as far as I—as yer brother and laird—am concerned."

Fiona stomped her foot again, one hand waving toward Duncan, while the other rested on her hip, as she faced her brother. "Even if he's *proven* his infidelity, before we even say our vows?"

Duncan held up a hand, palm out. "I'm no'—"

"Shut up, Finn!" she snapped.

"Ye'll marry the man, if I tell ye to marry the man!" Stewart roared.

Stomp. "I dinnae *want* to marry him!"

"I dinnae care!" her brother snapped back.

Duncan raised his other hand. "I dinnae want to marry her."

With a choked gasp, Fiona whirled on Duncan, angry tears in her eyes. "*Ye promised!*"

Finn jerked toward her, determined to ease her pain somehow.

But Skye beat him to it. As his heart broke to see Fiona's tears, her sister wrapped her in a hug.

Fee burrowed her face in Skye's shoulder. "I thought he loved me!" she wailed. "He swore it!"

Meeting Skye's eyes, Finn thought he saw hesitation—doubt?—there. As she absentmindedly rubbed her sister's back, she switched her gaze to Duncan, a thoughtful frown tugging at her lips.

"Mayhap…" Skye hummed. "Mayhap I was wrong, sister," she murmured cautiously.

Finn's breath caught.

Earlier, he'd wondered if Skye had been the reason for Fiona's current words. Now he wondered if she might be their salvation.

Against her sister's shoulder, Fiona mumbled, "What?"

Skye was still looking between Finn and Duncan, frowning. "Mayhap 'twas nae *Finn* who kissed me."

And in that one shining, horrible moment, it all made sense.

Evidently, Dunc figured it out as well, because he cursed under his breath and turned away, raking his fingers through his hair.

Slowly, Fiona straightened.

And Finn kept his attention locked on her sister. "I never kissed ye, Skye," he said clearly and distinctly.

Duncan muttered another nasty curse, as Skye nodded and turned Fiona in her arms. With her hands on Fee's shoulders, she took a deep breath.

"I am sorry for causing ye this pain, Fiona."

"I dinnae understand."

Skye winced. "They're…identical."

It felt as if the entire room held its breath. Finn knew he wasn't the only one watching as Fiona's expression eased from a frown, and her confusion cleared.

"Do ye think… Is it possible 'twas *Duncan* who kissed ye? Both times? No' Finn?"

As Skye winced again and nodded, Finn's heart bloomed with hope.

That's what all this was about! Dunc had confessed to kissing a "bonny lass" in the stables—days ago, and then again this morn. Had that been *Skye*? Who'd then run to Fiona with a story of *Finn* being unfaithful?

As quickly as his mood had sunk, Finn felt the bands around his chest easing.

"What in *damnation* is going on here?" Stewart roared.

Nessa began, "It appears Fiona believes *Finn* to be the one who kissed her sister—"

Fiona interrupted when she whirled on the identical men. One long, graceful finger jabbed at the air between them. "Which one of ye is Duncan?"

With his back still to the group, Duncan muttered, "*Shite*," and raised his hand.

And Finn smiled.

When he glanced back at Fiona, she was watching him, and his smile grew.

"I should've kenned yer smile," she murmured. Then she straightened. "Did ye kiss my sister?"

Still smiling, Finn shook his head.

She planted her hands on her hips and glared at Duncan. "Did *ye*?"

Proving he must've been watching the proceedings after all, Dunc's shoulders slumped. "St. Simon forgive me, *aye*."

Finn was ready to step forward, to sweep her into his arms. He had *every* intention of carrying her up those stairs to his room, tossing her on the bed, and pinning her under him while he explained the whole convoluted situation.

But Stewart obviously wasn't convinced. "So which one of these men did ye sleep with?"

Skye lifted a finger. "I was sleeping in the stable when one of them—Duncan, I suppose—"

"Nay, no' *ye*," her brother snapped. "I meant *sleep with* as a euphemism, because I refuse to think of my baby sister fooking." He shook his head as he glared at Fiona. "One of these two men came to *ye*, and before I betroth ye to him, I have to ken which one."

Her hands on her hips, Fiona narrowed her eyes at her brother. "Which one I fooked—I mean, the one I *gave myself to in a physical manifestation of our love*?" she finished in a treacly voice.

"Aye," Stewart said weakly. "That."

Finn smiled. Right up until her next words wiped it off his lips.

"He had a large freckle on his cock."

"What?" Stewart choked.

"The man I *slept with* had a large freckle on his cock," Fiona repeated, slower and louder.

"His...*cock*?" her brother repeated.

She nodded. "Ye ken, his male copulatory organ?"

"I ken what a cock is!" Stewart snapped. "But no' what *his* cock looks like."

Nessa cleared her throat. "Ye have a pet rooster, Finn?"

Before anyone could set her straight, Stewart whirled on Finn. "Lift yer kilt," the MacIan laird commanded.

Torn between shock and laughter, Finn jerked back. "*Why?*"

"So we can see if ye have a freckle!" Stewart bellowed, as if this were all perfectly logical.

The laughter was beginning to win out now, threatening to crawl up Finn's throat and choke him with it. They were standing in the middle of the great hall, and as this completely ridiculous scene had played out, more and more of the Oliphants had gathered.

And Stewart MacIan wanted Finn to lift his kilt and show everyone his cock.

Oh well. If it means marrying Fiona...

Finn turned to his twin brother. "Do ye have a freckle on yer cock?"

Dunc shrugged. "I've never checked," he said drily. "But if it means no' having to marry the woman ye love..."

With a sigh, Duncan reached down, grasped the bottom edge of his kilt, and lifted it.

Unwilling to have his brother prove the braver, Finn did the same.

And as he held his kilt high, around them, gasps, murmurs and titters filled the great hall, he met Fiona's eyes and tried to hold in his chuckles.

Her gaze dropped to their kilts, then lower still, as Finn and his brother stood there, holding their kilts aloft, bollocks dangling in the breeze.

Nessa made a little strangled noise of laughter, and Finn just hoped she wasn't sketching notes for her *Illustrated Bible of Coital Positions, Exhibited in a Variety of Embroidered Threads with Interesting Anecdotes, by A Lady.*

Duncan's eyes rolled toward the ceiling, and he muttered something about humiliation.

But Fiona...?

Fiona was staring at Finn's cock.

And as Finn's smile grew, he felt himself growing hard in response. Her eyes were locked on his cock, and her lips parted.

Was she short of breath?

That was *definitely* a flush working its way up her cheeks, but one of excitement, not embarrassment.

When she licked her lips, Finn damn near groaned in satisfaction.

She jerked toward him, even as her gaze snapped up to his. "That's him," she whispered hoarsely.

Her brother stirred. "Fiona?"

Fiona held Finn's gaze, the *want* and desperation plainly evident. "That's him," she repeated. "That's the man I'm going to marry."

Finn didn't wait for Stewart's approval, but dropped his kilt with a, *"Thank God!"* As he stepped forward, he slammed Dunc on the shoulder. "Thanks for yer help."

Before anyone else could react, he'd reached Fiona in two strides, bent, and scooped her up. She felt warm. She was certainly breathing heavily and didn't object at all as he rested her against his shoulder.

"I love ye, Fee," he murmured down at her.

It was clear she was struggling to think through the haze of desire clouding her eyes. "I— Oh, good." She licked her lips again, and he decided the action must've been directly linked to his cock, judging from the way that member stiffened even *further*.

As he took his first step toward the stairs, her sister blurted, "Where are ye going?"

Finn turned, but continued to walk backward as he explained, too anxious to get Fiona back upstairs to stop. "If ye think I endured that little farce, just to meekly tuck myself in and sit down to luncheon, ye're as mad as our resident musical ghost."

"Dooooooom!" Aunt Agatha hollered gleefully.

At that, Finn *did* stop, but only to readjust his hold on Fiona and nod to her brother. "We'll be in the solar in an hour, Laird MacIan," he said respectfully. "I'd suggest ye be there as well with yer betrothal papers."

Stewart opened his mouth, and just in case the man planned to object—or pass judgement on *how* Finn intended to pass the next hour—Finn explained.

"Fiona is mine." He dropped his gaze to hers and smiled. "She was mine since I met her. She was mine in every way but legally last night, and she'll be mine for the rest of our lives."

And before she could do more than whisper a breathless, "Oh my," he'd reached the stairs and was bounding up them, sweeping her up behind him, determined to make the most of the coming hour.

After all, they had a wedding to plan.

FIONA STRETCHED LANGUIDLY as Finn pulled the rest of her gown off her legs. Somehow, in their frantic love-making, the silk had gotten bunched around her waist.

Actually, there was no *somehow* about it; she knew exactly how it had happened. As soon as Finn had kicked the door shut behind them, *she'd* been the one to pull his lips down to hers. *She'd* been the one to slide down his body, to press herself against him, to grind her hips against his hardness.

He'd pretty much taken over from there.

Long story short, her gown's ties had ripped, she was missing a shoe, and Finn was still wearing his belt...but no plaid.

Now that they were both satisfied—and so quickly, too!—he was smiling as he dropped his belt atop the pile of kilt, then crawled back into bed with her.

"I love ye, Fee," he repeated, as he took her in his arms.

Suddenly embarrassed—not at her nudity, but at his words—she buried her face in his shoulder. "I am so sorry I doubted ye, my love."

She could hear the smile in his voice when he replied. " 'Twas an honest mistake."

" 'Twas a comedy of errors," she corrected in a muffled voice.

"Skye dinnae ken I had an identical brother, did she?" When Fiona shook her head, he shrugged. "Well then, 'twas an honest mistake. Just this morning, Duncan was telling me about the lass he'd kissed in the stable, but he hadn't met ye yet, so he had nae idea what ye—or Skye—looked like."

He was being so *charming* about this!

Blowing out a breath, she pushed herself up so she was balanced on her palms and frowning down at him.

"I was *so angry*, Finn, at the thought of ye betraying me. I shouldnae have doubted ye, even though my sister said—"

He cut her off by placing a callused fingertip on her lips. "Fee, ye had a right to be angry. But ye have my word that ye, and ye alone, hold my heart. I'll never betray ye; I'll never even look at another woman with want. Even if she's identical to ye."

When he smiled, her heart melted.

"Even..." Swallowing, she sat up completely, at ease with her nudity around him. "Even when my body is swollen and ugly with bairn?"

Slowly, his smile bloomed, and he dropped his hand to her stomach, while the other reached for her hip to trace small circles against her skin.

"Love," he said in a serious voice, " 'twill be *my* bairn ye'll carry. And the thought of ye carrying my bairn—*our* child—is the most arousing thing I can imagine."

Oh.

Judging from the way his member was stiffening again, he wasn't lying.

Her attention dropped to that male hardness...and his freckle.

"Do ye think..." She licked her lips and heard him suck in a breath. "Do ye think we'll have a bairn first, and ye'll be the next laird?"

His cock *was* getting hard, wasn't it?

But when he lifted his hand to her chin, turning her attention back to his eyes, she saw sincerity mixed with the desire in his gaze.

"Fiona MacIan, ye're going to be my wife. Because I want *ye*. I want *yer* children. I dinnae care if ye bear a son and I become the next laird, or if that headache goes to one of my brothers. *Ye're* the one I care about."

His words were everything she'd ever dreamed a man might say to her.

"Oh, Finn," she whispered, her heart swelling, at the same time warmth and wetness pooled between her thighs.

Again.

Giving into temptation, she leaned down and kissed him.

This wasn't the kiss they'd shared earlier; hot and desperate. This one was sweet and tender, and Fiona did her best to convey just how much he really meant to her.

When she pulled back, his eyes were serious. "What was that for?"

"That was to show ye"—she dropped a kiss to his nose—"that I love ye." A kiss on his chin. "I love everything about ye."

Shifting to her knees, she leaned forward to be able to press her lips to that delicious spot at the base of his throat.

"I love yer honor." She couldn't resist another kiss there, at his top of his chest. "I love yer charm."

Her lips moved first to one nipple, then the other, and when her tongue circled one of his the same as he'd done to hers, he sucked in a breath.

Peeking lower, she could see his cock standing stiffly at attention, and his hands were curled into fists in the bedclothes.

She dragged her tongue down his stomach, stopping at his navel. "I love *ye*, Finn Oliphant, and I cannae wait to become yer wife," she murmured against his skin.

"Fiona…!" he groaned in a pleading voice.

So she was smiling as she reached the place where she'd wanted to be.

Had it been just last night she'd stared at his velvety-smooth, steel-hard member—complete with freckle!—and wondered what it would taste like?

Well, now she would know.

Cupping his bollocks, she grasped his shaft with her other hand and turned to grin at him.

"Are ye determined to drain me in the next hour, lass?" he managed in a choked whisper.

Ah, that was right. They had to meet Stewart to sign the marriage contract in...less than an hour now.

But that left her plenty of time to explore her soon-to-be-husband. Her lips tugged upward naughtily.

"Every last drop, my love."

"St. Ninian's tits, but I do love ye, Fiona."

"Now and forever, Finn?"

In her hand, his cock throbbed, a pulse which matched the aching in her core. His hand dropped to her arse, his fingers curling under and around, finding the place she needed his touch.

But he held her gaze. "Now and forever, love."

Smiling, she lowered her lips to him.

EPILOGUE

Duncan stood, arms folded, watching the revelers at his brother's wedding.

Who knew a ceremony could be arranged so quickly?

Da had insisted on the finest foods and ale, so poor Moira had been running about for a sennight arranging things. There were fiddlers and pipers, and fresh flowers galore, and so much merriment you could cut your teeth on it.

'Tis sickening!

If Duncan ever got married—and that was a big *if*, although he wasn't so opposed as his brother Kiergan—he'd make do with something simple, and hope his betrothed felt the same.

Of course, he knew Finn fairly well. They'd shared a womb, after all. And they'd had even more times to speak this week, so Duncan had discovered his brother would've been fine with a simple ceremony as well, if it meant claiming Fiona as his own much sooner.

Or mayhap he might've happily been able to prolong the waiting, had he at least had *access* to his Fiona. But in the last sennight, Duncan's twin had been bedding down at the forge with him, rolled in their plaids on a makeshift pallet, because the bride's *sister* refused to vacate their room long enough to allow Finn to sneak in.

That same sister now spun Fiona—the newly forged Fiona

Oliphant, that was—happily, their identical hair braided with identical flowers, wearing identical smiles.

Aye, they were as alike as he and Finn were, but only a fool would mistake them for one another.

Where his brother's new wife was always giddy and bubbly, blurting out her thoughts and caring for others, her twin was thoughtful and quiet.

Or mayhap she was only that way with him.

She *had* punched him, after all.

Unconsciously, Duncan raised his fingertips to his left cheekbone. Her blow hadn't left a bruise, but he wasn't going to forget the way her blue eyes had spat fire at him as she'd awoken, swinging her fists.

She'd been *stunning*, and not just in the slam-ye-in-the-head-with-a-caber kind of stunning.

His scowl deepened, and he dropped his hand, reaching instead for a flagon of ale on a nearby table. There was less than a mouthful left, and he drained it easily.

It wasn't enough.

He suspected there would *never* be enough ale to forget the shame of kissing her without her permission. Or discovering she was his brother's betrothed.

And *then* discovering she wasn't the Lady Fiona at all, but her identical twin sister—

St. Simon's big toe, was there no more ale in this place?

With a growl, he slammed the flagon back on the table, wishing he could wash away the shame—the *desire*—just as easily.

"Are ye thirsty?"

He spun around.

There she was—*Skye*—holding two flagons of ale. He peered at her, then at the flagon.

" 'Tis poisoned?"

A smile flitted across her lips, but was gone before his body could react. "If I wanted to kill ye, Dunc, I'd no' do it with poison."

Dunc. He'd always hated when his brothers called him that—sounded too close to *Duck*—but when *she* said it...?

Well, when Skye Maclan called him that, it didn't sound quite so bad.

Cautiously, he took the ale. Sniffing it, he decided she was likely telling the truth and it was safe, so he took a sip.

She'd turned back to the celebration, but hadn't left his side.

Swallowing, he cast about for a topic of conversation. One which didn't have anything to do with her anger, his gaffe, or the desire they'd both felt when they'd touched one another.

"How *would* ye do it?" he blurted out.

"Do what?"

She wasn't looking at him, which made it easier. "How would ye kill me, if ye wanted to?"

Her lips curled into that enigmatic smile once more, her attention on the revelry. "If I wanted to kill ye, Dunc, I'd do it with a blade." Slowly, she turned to him, that smile still in place. "And I'd do it facing ye."

St. Simon, bless me!

The lass looked as if she meant what she said. But surely a *Lady* wouldn't know anything about blades or swordplay?

Duncan hurriedly took another drink, noticing she still cradled her flagon. He'd made more than a few blades in his day, but preferred not to use them. Oh, he'd trained, the same as all of his brothers, but he would rather use his wits to get out of danger. Besides, the size of his shoulders usually scared any would-be attackers away.

That thought led to another, and he took a few steps away from her. "Do ye have reason to want to kill me?"

She shrugged, then lifted her flagon to her lips.

And that was enough of an answer, wasn't it?

He'd insulted her, and she'd likely not forget that in a hurry.

"When are ye going home?" he blurted, then hid his wince by turning to thump the ale down on the table beside him. He'd apparently had enough, if he was asking such bald questions.

And apparently, she knew it, judging from the dryness of her tone. "Soon, I suspect. Stewart will want to see Fiona settled as Finn's wife, but his own wife is expecting his heir soon, so we'll likely hurry back. Ye'll be rid of me soon enough."

Soon enough?

Not likely.

Until she left, he wouldn't be able to forget how much of a fool he'd been.

And wouldn't be able to stop wondering when she'd strike.

So he cleared his throat, his decision made.

"I'll likely be saying my goodbyes even sooner."

"Oh?" She was just being polite, he was certain.

Still, he nodded, already mentally preparing his exit. "I have a journey to Eriboll. My master has sent me to pick up some pieces, and I expect to be gone—gone for some time."

Exchanging the jewelry for coin would take little time, but he'd do his best to linger in Eriboll, if it meant not having to see Skye again...and keeping his body intact.

The noise she made at the news, however, was speculative as she watched her sister and his brother dancing. Finally, she nodded.

"Well, yer journey will take ye near MacIan land. I'm certain my brother will welcome yer visit, if ye'd like to stop."

"Thank ye, but—" *But nay.* He searched for a politer answer. "I'll —I'll consider it."

"Well, then..."

To his surprise, she shifted her flagon to one hand and thrust the other one toward him. As if they were men. As if they were men, who'd just closed a deal.

Hesitating more than a little, he finally took her hand in his.

It wasn't the traditional forearm grip he and his brothers shared. But it caused a warmth to jolt up his arm so quickly, he sucked in a breath.

She must not have felt it, because she just nodded.

"Safe journey, Dunc."

And then she dropped his hand, offered him the slightest smile —was there mockery in it?—and turned away.

As she crossed the hall to her brother, Duncan cradled his hand against his chest, staring after her. Trying not to admire the way her arse moved under that silk gown.

And failing.

He squeezed his eyes shut.

I'll leave tomorrow. I'll sleep in the rain and the cold. I'll walk if the pain in my feet will drive out the memory of her.

But when he opened his eyes and saw her throw her head back, he knew it was a futile effort. Skye MacIan—and the anger they shared—couldn't be dismissed so easily.

Shite.

AUTHOR'S NOTE

AUTHOR'S NOTE
On Historical Accuracy

Listen, this is the place where I talk history, right? Usually, I mention how the great kilt didn't become a *thing* until the 16th century, but how we're going to ignore that because *OMG* heroes in kilts, am I right?

Or I talk about the location of the book or the famous players, or even the social history like—I dunno—leprosy or painting techniques or whatever.

But…

But surely you realized this book wasn't intended to be factually accurate. About *anything*.

I purposefully didn't even give you a good idea on the time period, because I wanted this series to be vague and hilarious and more than a little irreverent. The best you're going to get out of me is the location of the Oliphant lands; north of Inverness and south of Wick, which is pretty darn vague.

So… Sorry. I have no history lesson for you here. There's plenty of stuff in this book which I didn't even intend to be accurate. Like coffee. And ghosts which warn of the cheese turning. And pretty much the entire plot set-up.

I set out to write a comedy as near to something Shakespeare might write—complete with dick and fart jokes—as possible. I think I nailed it, but maybe that's because I have an immature sense of humor. I'd love to know what you think! Find me on Facebook or email me at Caroline@CarolineLeeRomance.com and let me know!

If you enjoyed the book, and are curious about the rest of the Oliphant lads, you're in luck; Duncan's story is ready for you! Keep reading for a sneak peek at *Scot on her Trail*!

But first, I want to offer you a personal invitation to my reader group. If you're on Facebook, I hope you'll consider joining. It's where I post all the best book news first, and you'll be able to get to know me personally. My Cohort is also instrumental in helping me name characters and choose covers! So stop on by!

And now, for Duncan and Skye...

SNEAK PEEK

We know how Duncan Oliphant met Skye MacIan…and we know it wasn't exactly a great memory for either. Well, *Skye* might not have minded that eye-full she got of Dunc, standing in the great hall with his kilt up around his ears. And Duncan *definitely* didn't mind that searing kiss they shared…up until she punched him.

But clearly they're unsuited for one another, right? Let's see what happens when they meet again in *Scot on Her Trail...*

———

When he spied the flash of crimson in the hedge by the side of the road, he slowed his horse. Frowning, he glanced about.

The road was bordered by a copse of fir trees on one side, and brambles on the other. No reason for there to be anything *crimson* out here.

Not seeing any danger, he cautiously edged his horse closer.

There, in the ditch beside the road…

Why was there *silk* piled there?

And…was that a hand? A *woman's* hand?

Before his mind could really process what he was seeing, Duncan was out of his saddle, sprinting for the flash of red silk.

Aye, 'twas a woman!

Dropping to his knees beside her, Duncan realized his hands were curled into fists. *St. Simon's hairy bollocks*, but he felt useless! He forced himself to breathe as he studied her.

She was lying on her side, curled up as if in pain. Her brown hair —such luscious curls—fell freely around her face and shoulders, before being ground into the dirt beneath her.

What had happened?

He forced his hands to open, to reach gently for her. His finger-tips skimmed her arm, her shoulder, as gently as he handled his gold and silver. She made no sound or movement, and he couldn't tell if anything was broken.

There was no blood though, which he decided was a good sign.

Where in damnation was her horse?

Duncan dragged his gaze away from her to scan the road and the trees once more. *Naught.* And she was still just as unmoving.

He needed to turn her over to check for injuries he couldn't see.

Bending, he slid his left arm under her shoulder, tilting her head so her hair fell away from her jaw, which was clenched, as if she were conscious and in pain, but her eyes were shut.

"*Shh, lass,*" he whispered gently, not sure if she could hear him. " 'Twill be aright. I've got ye."

Gently, he straightened and sat on his heels, pulling her with him. She turned in his arms, her left arm still hidden under her body, and slowly opened her eyes.

He almost dropped her.

'Twas Skye MacIan; the woman who had been haunting his dreams for weeks.

"Where—where am I?" she murmured, lifting her right hand to her head, while her left swept around toward his side. Duncan felt something sharp poking him under his ribs, and just as soon as he could make his brain work, he'd figure out what that was.

But for now, *Skye MacIan* was in his arms, in the middle of the road, miles from her home.

"Lass?" he prompted her.

"I had the strangest—" She got a good look at him, and suddenly her eyes opened wide.

Trying to be helpful, he supplied, "Dream? Accident? Spiritual encounter with a saintly apparition? Gastrointestinal difficulties?"

Her eyes widened further. "*Shite*."

Ah, so it *was* the gastrointestinal one. "Shite?"

She shook her head, and the sudden sharp prick in his side made him frown.

"Shite*shiteshitefook*."

Duncan's brows went up at her vocabulary. " 'Tis good to see ye too," he said drily.

"Put me down, ye great oaf."

Oaf?

He shook his head, realizing he was quite enjoying having her there in his arms. "Nay, no' until I ken ye're no' hurt."

"I'm no' hurt, but *ye* will be, if ye dinnae release me."

The way her gaze darted over his shoulder, then down to his side, had Duncan glancing down as well.

She was holding a dagger. A dagger which was currently pressed against his ribs, aimed for his heart.

"What are ye doing?" he asked mildly.

"I *was* robbing ye."

"What…alone?"

"Nay, laddie, no' alone," came the deep rumble from behind him.

Instinctively, he tried to shield the lass in his arms from whatever threat behind him might be, but when she jabbed him with that damn dagger again, he jerked back and loosened his hold on her.

When she kicked at him, Duncan fell back on his arse as she tried to scramble away from him. "By St. Simon's gilded piss, *what* in damnation are ye doing, lass?"

Even her frown was adorable. "Getting stuck in this bloody ridiculous gown, is what I'm doing," she muttered, her dagger not leaving her hand.

He was reaching for her, the primal need to help her overriding whatever threat she might claim to pose, when a shadow fell over them both.

"Here," the shadow grunted, manifesting a *huge* hand and reaching down to offer help to Skye.

She took the *shadow's* help, damn him, and stood with only a few curses.

And to Duncan's surprise, he found the idea of Skye MacIan—a proper lady—*cursing*, to be strangely arousing.

The sound of steel being drawn from leather dragged his attention away from Skye, who was trying to brush the dirt from her skirts. That silk molded to her in the most *interesting* ways, but the scowling older man with the sword made it difficult to focus on her.

"Ye're no' supposed to *cuddle* with her, ye *crumpety* clot-heid!"

Crumpety?

"I was no' cuddling with Skye," Duncan said, with an affronted air as he pushed himself to his feet. "I needed to make sure she wasnae hurt."

The older man jabbed forward with his sword, enough to make Duncan step back, but not close enough to hurt him. "Ye're no' supposed to ken her *name* either." He scowled at the mustached man by his side. "Pierre dinnae say aught of *kenning* ye."

At the accusation in his tone, the other man shrugged. "*Regardez combien son sac est lourd!*"

Duncan knew some French, thanks to his years studying with Master Claire. His right hand twitched toward his purse, while the other rested on the hilt of his sword.

"Ye really *are* bandits?"

The youngest member of their group shook his head. "We're *highwaymen.*"

"Oh, well, my apologies then." Duncan cut a glance at Skye, while also attempting to keep the other men in his sights. "Ye're a part of this?"

With a sigh, she jammed her dagger back in its sheath and

planted her fists on her hips. "I'm their *leader*, ye bumbled-headed clackdish. And 'twas rotten luck Pierre chose *ye* as our next mark."

The MacIan Laird's sister was a highwayman?

*Nay. Look at her in that gown. She's verra much a highway*woman.

One he wouldn't mind cuddling with again.

Ready to find out if Skye succeeds in robbing Dunc of his gold? Grab your copy of *Scot on Her Trail* today!

Thanks so much for reading *A Scot Mess*! If you enjoyed the story, please consider leaving a review—even a short one! Reviews are bread and butter to an author like me, and I read each one.

And if this book brought you joy, I would so appreciate you sharing this book with your friends and family! You can share this link directly in email or on social media: mybook.to/AScotMess

And remember, you can always get a free book by signing up for my newsletter at www.CarolineLeeRomance.com!

ABOUT THE AUTHOR

Caroline Lee has been reading romance for so long that her fourth-grade teacher used to make her cover her books with paper jackets. But it wasn't until she (mostly) grew up that she realized she could *write* it too. So she did.

Caroline is living her own little Happily Ever After in NC with her husband, sons, and new daughter, Princess Wiggles. And while she doesn't so much "suffer" from Pittakionophobia as think that all you people who enjoy touching Band-Aids and stickers are the real weirdos, she *does* adore rodents, and never met a wine she didn't like. Caroline was named Time Magazine's Person of the Year in 2006 (along with everyone else) and is really quite funny in person. Promise.

You can find her at www.CarolineLeeRomance.com.

The Calendar Girls' Ranch (6 books)

Click **here** to find a complete list of Caroline's books.

*Sign up for Caroline's Newsletter to receive exclusive content and freebies, as well as first dibs on her books! Or if newsletters aren't your thing, follow her on **Bookbub** for a quick, concise new release alert every time she publishes a book!*

Made in the USA
Middletown, DE
12 March 2024

51124962R10089